Beside him, the nurserymaid ground her teeth hard enough for him to hear it.

The girls shot her glances of triumph and strolled into the parlor.

"How dare you counter my directions." Her tone, though low, held so much fury Gordon expected sparks to fly from the ends of her hair. "I am their governess, and they need to view me as an authority."

"I am their uncle, and they need to view me as an authority." He made his own voice as cool as he could to emphasize her hot fury. "Since I am their legal guardian, I believe what I say has precedent over what you say."

"Since you couldn't be bothered to come home for months," she shot back, practically hissing, "you seem to have relinquished your right to barge in here and start telling them and me what to do."

"I couldn't get here faster."

"Or ensure that we had money for wages and other fees?"

"I didn't realize—"

"The only reason we have had food to eat and clothes the girls fit into is because their parents had good credit and the vendors knew they'd be paid eventually. The music teacher and others haven't been quite so accommodating, nor were servants."

"You're here."

"I"—she slapped her hands onto her hips—"cared too much about the girls to desert them in their time of need."

Award-winning author **LAURIE ALICE EAKES** has always loved books. When she ran out of available stories to entertain and encourage her, she began creating her own tales of love and adventure. In 2006 she celebrated the publication of her first hardcover novel. Much to her astonishment and delight, it won the National Readers Choice Award. Since then, she has sold eight more historical romances. A graduate of Asbury College and Seton Hill University, she lives in Texas with her husband and sundry animals.

Books by Laurie Alice Eakes

HEARTSONG PRESENTS
HP791—Better Than Gold
HP880—The Glassblower
HP899—The Heiress

The Newcomer

Laurie Alice Eakes

Heartsong Presents

To my nieces, who are precious to me.

A note from the Author:
I love to hear from my readers! You may correspond with me by writing:

Laurie Alice Eakes
Author Relations
PO Box 721
Uhrichsville, OH 44683

ISBN 978-1-60260-914-3

THE NEWCOMER

All scripture quotations are taken from the King James Version of the Bible.

All of the characters and events in this book are fictitious. Any resemblance to actual persons, living or dead, or to actual events is purely coincidental.

Our mission is to publish and distribute inspirational products offering exceptional value and biblical encouragement to the masses.

PRINTED IN THE U.S.A.

one

A flick of the turkey-feather brush dislodged dust, an invitation to a picnic, and a gray and silver–striped kitten from the parlor mantel. The invitation wedged itself in the fire screen, where it stuck out like a child's insolent tongue. The kitten displaced a picture of a solemn-faced couple in wedding garb.

Sneezing from the flying dust, Marigold McCorkle caught the picture before it smashed on the hearth. In the foyer, the kitten squealed then vanished into the library. For a moment, the dust whirled about in the afternoon sunshine, like a taunt, then settled over the carved mahogany mantel once again.

"That never happens when Mrs. Cromwell dusts." The observation came from nine-year-old Beryl Chambers. She stood in the parlor doorway, her long-fingered hands on her hips, and every aspect of her appearance—from the white straw hat perched atop her glossy, blond pigtails to her white dress banded with dove gray ribbons to her white button shoes—was in place, spotless, and unblemished.

In contrast, Marigold knew her flaming hair was bursting from its pins in a hundred directions. Her plain, gray dress bore the marks of stove blackening on one sleeve, and white was no longer a word one could apply to her apron.

"You should go slower," Beryl continued. "That way the feathers collect the dust instead of just making it fly around. Would you like my handkerchief?"

It, too, would be pristine.

Marigold sighed. "No, thank you. I need to go change my

dress and wash a bit. Where's your sister?"

"Sulking in the garden." Beryl stuck her pert nose in the air. "She's such a baby."

"She's only six."

And worried about the new person about to spring upon her life.

"You need to be patient with her." Marigold dusted the silver picture frame with a clean corner of her apron and set it on the mantel beside the clock. That instrument ticked by the minutes in an ominous reminder that the train was due in less than an hour, and she'd better get herself up to her room and into clean clothes. Just because her original duties as the girls' nurserymaid had also turned into governess and housemaid since the death of their parents, didn't mean she could meet the new master of the house looking like a duster if someone turned her on her head.

"Is she ready for your uncle?" Marigold asked.

"No, she wouldn't let me help her, and Mrs. Cromwell is busy making dinner."

"Then will you please fetch her inside and send her up to the nursery?" Marigold let her gaze dance around the room in search of anything in need of dusting, polishing, straightening.

Every stick of furniture glowed with the patina of fine wood. The aroma of beeswax and lemon scented the air from the polishing, along with the fragrance of some late-blooming roses cut out of the garden and set in tall, crystal vases. White puff balls of hydrangeas appeared to float in their shimmering glass bowls set amid framed photographs, china figurines, and some small, wooden carvings that covered every available surface. Above her, the ceiling fan spun in a lazy circle, the moving air countering the warmth of the August sunshine spilling in through draperies open to welcome home the new owner of the house.

"It will do," Marigold decided and headed for the doorway.

Beryl still stood there, her hands now clutched together at her waist.

"What is it, child?" Marigold asked.

"I'm not a child." Beryl's suddenly trembling lower lip belied her claim. "I'll be ten in another month."

"I beg your pardon. I'm more than twice your age, and my father still calls me 'child.' You, of course, are quite grown up and don't need me at all, but how may I help you?"

"It's Ruby." Beryl blinked her huge, blue eyes—eyes that looked a little glassy. "She's afraid Uncle Gordon isn't very nice."

So was Marigold. After all, how good could a man be when he took three months to come care for his orphaned nieces? For herself, she was prepared to heartily dislike him. Those three months of not responding to her pleading telegrams to return to Cape May, New Jersey, had cost her dearly.

She offered Beryl an encouraging smile she feared wouldn't ring true. "He's nice enough to come home, isn't he? And his telegram was kind."

No, kind wasn't the right word. Polite and promising generosity, yes. Considerate, barely. Kind? Only if implying he could make up for his long and unexplained absence by paying her extra wages was kind.

She clenched her fingers. A crack like a shot burst through the room. A sharp pain gouged Marigold's hand.

"Miss Marigold," Beryl cried, "you're bleeding!"

"I am?" Marigold glanced down to discover blood indeed trickling from her palm. She'd broken the handle of the feather duster, and the sharp ends of the split wood dug into her flesh. "I'd better go wash this. Will you please fetch Ruby upstairs? We can talk while I'm washing up and changing my dress."

"We can't talk about Ruby being scared." Beryl turned away. "It'll make her feel bad."

"Then we'll pretend we're talking about you."

Marigold wanted to hug the child, but Beryl would never tolerate a smudge or wrinkle to her appearance. She was already moving away, anyhow. As she reached the door, she slipped her hand into a tiny white pocketbook and withdrew what was, without a doubt now, a spotless, white handkerchief with a black border to remind everyone of her recent loss.

"Poor babies," Marigold murmured.

Her own eyes burning—possibly from the dust—she gathered up her skirt and raced up the steps. Fifty-three minutes were not enough to wash, change her dress, and do something reasonable with her hair, plus tidy Ruby.

"Please don't let anything else interfere," Marigold prayed, meaning she hoped Mrs. Cromwell, the cook and housekeeper, wouldn't request her assistance for anything.

Marigold darted into the room the girls' parents had converted to a nursery bathroom. She longed for a bath after cleaning all morning in the sticky, New Jersey August heat. She settled for a wash in the deep bowl of the sink then pulled the remaining pins from her hair. It cascaded around her face and shoulders in carroty curls so tight most combs broke trying to make their way through. It would have to wait for renewed pinning until after she donned a clean dress and saw to Ruby.

Marigold's clothes lay on her bed in the room reserved for the governess, though she'd only been hired as a nursemaid fifteen months earlier. White muslin dotted with tiny violets fluttered over her head, sending her hair floating outward, then settled onto her petticoats. Twisting a bit, she managed to get the buttons into their holes, then reached for her buttonhook to remove the heavy black footgear she wore while doing housework and don the pretty white ones for dress apparel.

She'd gotten off the first pair and stood in her stocking feet, reaching for the second pair in her wardrobe, when Ruby scuffed through the bedroom door and Mrs. Cromwell called up the back steps for assistance lifting the roasting pan out of the oven.

"Now," the housekeeper emphasized.

Marigold eyed Ruby's smudged chin, grubby hands, and

torn dress with its suspiciously squirming pocket. "If that's not the kitten in there, take it outside immediately. If it is, sit on the chair there and wait for me. I'll be back in a moment."

"It's Dahlia," Ruby mumbled. Her voice had grown too soft since her parents' death. "She was sitting on Daddy's desk, and he doesn't like her there."

"If you hold on to her, Dahlia is in good hands." Marigold tousled Ruby's golden hair, which would also need to be braided again, then dashed out the door and down the rear staircase to the kitchen.

"Do you have a clean apron? I don't want to soil this dress."

"You know where they are." Mrs. Cromwell pointed her salt-and-pepper bun toward the pantry door.

On a row of hooks, spotless aprons hung. Marigold snatched one down and yanked the strings so hard around her trim waist that one parted from the apron.

"I'll sew it back on," she said before the housekeeper could scold her.

"If you go more slowly," Mrs. Cromwell admonished, "that sort of thing won't happen." She gave the apron a narrow-eyed glance. "That was the one you mended last week."

So she didn't sew any better than she dusted.

Marigold sighed and, with the speed of a turtle crossing the road, removed another apron from a hook and tied it behind her.

"My roast is drying out." Mrs. Cromwell tapped the toe of her heavy brogan, shoes that reminded Marigold of her great-grandmother Bridget. "Can't be waiting all day."

"No, ma'am." Marigold snatched up towels folded for the purpose of protecting one's hands from the heat and opened the oven door. Steam smelling of roasted beef, potatoes, carrots, and sweet onions billowed toward her. Her stomach growled. Her mouth watered. Her hair sprang into wilder curls, as it tumbled around her face, tickling her nose and tangling with her eyelashes.

She blew the hair out of her face and hefted the huge

roasting pan onto the worktable, something Mrs. Cromwell was growing too frail to manage on her own. "Do you need anything else, ma'am?"

"No thank you, I can manage from here." Mrs. Cromwell frowned at Marigold. "But will you please tie your hair back before coming into my kitchen. As pretty as it is, we don't want to be eating it."

"Pretty?" Marigold laughed. "It's a fright, and you are a dear for saying otherwise." She kissed the old lady's wrinkled cheek then raced back up the steps.

"Slow down before you hurt yourself," Mrs. Cromwell called after her.

If only she had time to slow down. The train was due into the station in ten minutes. Even if Mr. Gordon Chambers disembarked last and waited for his luggage to be unloaded, experience with the train on a weekday, not as busy as the weekends, told Marigold he would arrive in half an hour at the most—and too possibly less. Cape May just wasn't large enough for getting anywhere to take long.

Marigold charged into her bedroom to gather up Ruby and take her for a wash and change of clothes. But Ruby no longer perched on the desk chair. Nor did she appear to be anywhere in the room or the bathroom. Marigold glanced into the girls' room. No Ruby appeared there either, though her dress, matching Beryl's, lay across her pink gingham coverlet.

"Ruby, where are you?" Marigold called. "Where—"

A thud and a cry from the schoolroom on the other side of the bathroom interrupted the query.

Marigold sprinted in that direction. She burst through the doorway in time to find Ruby lying on the floor beside an overturned chair and Dahlia, the kitten, glaring down at the scene from atop the bookcase.

"Are you all right?" Marigold dropped to her knees beside Ruby.

Ruby nodded but didn't move.

"Where are you hurt?" Marigold touched the child's head, seeking lumps. "Look at me, baby."

Ruby looked at her and gasped for air.

"She's just winded." Beryl marched into the room, stood on tiptoe, and plucked the kitten from the shelf. "You should know better than to climb onto chairs."

"I—know." Ruby managed to wheeze. "She was—crying to get down."

"Next time," Marigold admonished, "you ask someone taller to get her down, all right?"

Ruby nodded.

"Good. Are you in pain?" Marigold debated whether to call for a doctor. "Can you get up on your own?"

Ruby nodded again.

"Then let's get you dressed and your hair combed." Marigold took the girl's soft little hands in hers, noting a long scratch on one of them. "And clean up that scrape."

"You need to let Dahlia go when she wants to go." Beryl sighed. "You never learn."

"Beryl," Marigold said, "please go downstairs and see if Mrs. Cromwell needs your help setting the table."

"She doesn't." Beryl selected a book from the shelf and perched on the window seat. "I already did it."

"At least one of us is competent," Marigold muttered. Aloud she said, "Come along, Ruby."

"Yes, ma'am." Ruby sat up with no apparent difficulty.

Marigold helped her to her feet, then led her into the bathroom to wash her up, then to the girls' room to change Ruby's dress. Her hair, like Beryl's, brushed out with barely a snarl to slow the progress. It waved so prettily, Marigold was half tempted to leave it flowing down Ruby's back. But Beryl insisted that they have their hair braided and wear white ribbons tied around the ends. So Marigold sat on the dressing table stool and began the tedious task she'd performed that morning—twisting the child's waist-length tresses into smooth, even plaits.

Throughout the process, Ruby stood perfectly still. Marigold would have been pleased at such compliance, except Ruby had fought having her hair tended to only three months ago, right up to the day her parents, full of life and laughter and love for their children and one another, went out sailing on one of the boats the Chambers Excursion and Sailing Company owned and returned when the tide washed their bodies ashore. Now Marigold wished Ruby would squirm and complain, instead of playing like she was a breathing statue of a little girl.

Halfway through the second braid, Marigold remembered she was going to talk to the girls about not being frightened of their uncle. She supposed it was best. Just the sound of his name in her own head made her stomach curdle like cream left in the sun. Gordon. Too much like "gorgon," some mythological monster out of a fairy tale.

"Ouch!" Ruby exclaimed.

Marigold realized she'd tugged too hard on the child's hair, while thinking of Gordon Chambers and his tardy arrival home.

"I'm sorry. Almost done here." Marigold picked up the second ribbon and tied it around the end of the pigtail. "You look lovely. Let's go show Beryl."

Hand in hand, Marigold and Ruby started for the schoolroom. Before they reached it, Beryl's voice reached them. "He's here."

"Already?" Marigold peeked at the clock hanging on the schoolroom wall.

Either the train arrived early, or Mr. Gordon Chambers hadn't waited for his luggage.

Marigold's stomach felt as though it were wrapping itself around her sinking heart. In a few minutes, she would turn her charges over to a man who hadn't cared enough to come home in time for his twin brother's funeral, then waited another ten weeks to say whether or not he would return at all, and another two weeks to send a telegram announcing the train on which he would appear. As much as she wanted to get back to her own family in Hudson City, she hesitated at the top of the steps, each of her hands gripping that of one of the girls, her feet unwilling to carry her forward to open the front door to such a cold, indifferent man.

"These girls need lots of love, Lord," she mouthed toward the fanlight spreading its jewel-toned light over the foyer and steps. "They only have me, and I can't stay."

The doorbell chimed. It reverberated through Marigold's head like a hammer blow.

"Answer that." Mrs. Cromwell's voice drifted through the house.

"Follow me down," Marigold whispered. "And stand at the bottom of the steps and wait to be introduced. Remember to—"

The doorbell chimed twice in rapid succession.

"We know," Beryl said. "You'd better go."

"You don't want to get punished for making him wait," Ruby murmured.

No, it was Mr. Gordon Chambers who needed the chastisement for being late.

Marigold gripped the banister for support and ran down the carpeted steps and across the runner to the front door. Well-oiled, the bolt slid open without a sound. Marigold tugged the heavy portal open and stepped back to allow the man on the front porch to come inside.

Other than giving her a brusque nod, he didn't acknowledge her, but strode past to set his valise on the floor and crouch before the girls. "Beryl, Ruby, I'm your uncle Gordon and so very sorry it's taken me this long to get home." He spoke in a voice as warm and rich as lemon custard. "Will you forgive me now that I'm here to see to things?" He held out his hands—long-fingered hands like his brother's, like Beryl's, only his were bronzed and hard-looking.

The girls made no move to take his hands or even speak. Ruby stuck the first two fingers of her right hand into her mouth, and Beryl's right toe tapped against the carpet.

"It was inexcusable of me to stay away so long, wasn't it?" Mr. Chambers said.

Though Marigold only saw him in profile, she caught his smile and the way it creased the corner of his eye. Breath snagged in her throat. From the side, his resemblance to his brother made her blink. For a heartbeat, Gerald Chambers might have returned to them—but only for a heartbeat. A second glance showed Gordon's hair curled more, and his shoulders appeared broader, his arms more powerful.

Marigold inhaled to steady herself from the shock and switched her gaze to the girls. Their faces had paled, their eyes widened. Marigold half expected them to cry "Daddy," but they remained silent, motionless, possibly as stunned as she.

He took one of the girls' hands in each of his. "I'll make things as right for you as I can, I promise," he continued into the silence.

"You're not as handsome as Daddy," Beryl pronounced.

Marigold licked her dry lips. Beryl must prefer a more refined look. To Marigold, Gordon Chambers, at least in profile, outweighed his brother in attractiveness, at least to her, silly female that she was in that moment.

"Will you bring Mommy and Daddy back?" Ruby asked in her whispery voice.

"I wish I could, child." His voice roughened. "But since I can't, I'll make sure you have good people to take care of you."

Good people? Not him?

The doorbell announcing his arrival should have been an alarm.

Marigold clenched her teeth to keep herself from speaking out of turn.

Beryl stuck her pert little nose in the air. "We already have good people to take care of us, sir—Mrs. Cromwell and Miss Marigold."

"I see." Releasing the girls' hands, Mr. Chambers stood. "I know Mrs. Cromwell, but who is Miss Marigold?"

"She's right behind you," Beryl announced in a tone verging

close enough to insolent that Marigold would have to talk to her about respect.

But not now. At that moment, she found herself receiving Gordon Chambers' full attention. Eyes the brown of root beer swept over her from head to foot, from her unbound mop of hair to her unshod feet.

"Miss Marigold, I presume?" he drawled.

"Yes." Marigold's voice sounded as whispery as Ruby's.

"Then I am making the right decision, and no one here should be in charge of these children for much longer."

two

Gordon Chambers stared at the female in charge of his nieces and wondered how anyone thought her old enough, let alone responsible enough, to oversee the well-being of children whose parents were alive, let alone. . .dead.

His heart tripped over the last word, thoughts of the brother he hadn't seen in eleven years, the sister-in-law he'd never met. Careless actions had driven a continent-wide wedge between him and his family, and he wasn't prepared to let someone as young as he had been at that time remain in charge of Ruby and Beryl.

Which meant he couldn't go to Alaska as soon as he wanted.

He sighed. "You are Marigold—"

"McCorkle, yes. I came here fifteen months ago to be the girls' nurserymaid."

He expected her to bob a curtsy, as his nurserymaid had done with his parents when he was a boy. She remained upright and met his gaze with bold, green eyes.

"I've also taken on some of the duties of a governess," she added with a hint of censure, "since they haven't been able to continue their summer lessons."

"What summer lessons—" He stopped. "We'll discuss that later." He glanced around. "Which room was prepared for me?"

"Your old room," Beryl spoke up. "Mommy left it just as it was so you'd come home."

Ruby pulled her fingers from her mouth. "Just like we left Mommy and Daddy's room just like it is so they'll come home."

Miss McCorkle cleared her throat. Gordon thought he understood why. His own neck tightened.

He swallowed. "Well, you see, I did come. . .back here.

16

And I'm glad I'll have my room to go to." He tried to smile, though his lips felt stiff like the mouth on a mask. "Can someone bring me up hot water? From the smell of it, Mrs. Cromwell has dinner about ready, and I need to wash first."

"You don't need someone to bring up hot water," Beryl announced, her pert nose a bit elevated. "We have bathrooms."

"Hot water comes up from a reservoir in the kitchen," Miss McCorkle added.

"Thank you." He glanced at her, shuddered at her wild appearance, and picked up his valise. "I have a trunk back at the station. Will you send the coachman to fetch it?"

"We don't have a coachman no more," Ruby mumbled around the fingers in her mouth once again.

"Anymore," Beryl and Miss McCorkle said at the same time.

"That's right," Gordon said. "It's his day off, isn't it? That's why he couldn't come get me at the train station."

"No, that isn't why no one could come get you." Miss McCorkle's tone sounded as hard as railroad ties. "When Ruby said we don't have a coachman, she meant we don't have a coachman or any other staff except for Mrs. Cromwell and me."

"Why not?" He had to face her to see what her expression gave away beyond her words. "The last I knew, this house was overflowing with servants."

"It was until—" She glanced at the children. "Girls, go wash your hands and see if Mrs. Cromwell needs you to help her carry things into the dining room."

"Ruby can't carry anything." Beryl made a face. "She drops the plates and spills the water."

Miss McCorkle drew together brows as red as her hair. "Then help her sit in her chair and be quiet until we join you."

"But Uncle Gordon gives us orders now," Ruby protested in an undertone.

"I'm going to my room to make myself presentable for Mrs. Cromwell's dinner." Gordon smiled at the girls. "You may wait for me in the parlor, and Miss McCorkle can set the food on the table."

Beside him, the nurserymaid ground her teeth hard enough for him to hear it.

The girls shot her glances of triumph and strolled into the parlor.

"How dare you counter my directions." Her tone, though low, held so much fury Gordon expected sparks to fly from the ends of her hair. "I am their governess, and they need to view me as an authority."

"I am their uncle, and they need to view me as an authority." He made his own voice as cool as he could to emphasize her hot fury. "Since I am their legal guardian, I believe what I say has precedent over what you say."

"Since you couldn't be bothered to come home for months," she shot back, practically hissing, "you seem to have relinquished your right to barge in here and start telling them and me what to do."

"I couldn't get here faster."

"Or ensure that we had money for wages and other fees?"

"I didn't realize—"

"The only reason we have had food to eat and clothes the girls fit into is because their parents had good credit and the vendors knew they'd be paid eventually. The music teacher and others haven't been quite so accommodating, nor were servants."

"You're here."

"I"—she slapped her hands onto her hips—"cared too much about the girls to desert them in their time of need."

The twin daggers of her green eyes hit their target. Gordon's heart clenched. He flushed from his necktie to his hairline.

"We'll continue this discussion later." He bowed his head. "I seem to be in need of some information surrounding the deaths of my brother and sister-in-law."

"Indeed you are."

Her hauteur should have been the final straw of her ill-judged behaviors to compel him to dismiss her on the spot. Instead, he found the corners of his lips twitching. He suppressed the urge to grin at her insolence and gave her a brusque nod. "In the library after supper. I presume that hasn't changed?"

"No, sir." She seemed to grow smaller before his eyes. Even her hair looked less like the ruffled flower for which she was named. "If I may, um, may have a few minutes to finish dressing?" Her face turned the color of a New Mexico sunset, clashing with her hair. "I mean, my hair." She yanked on a strand, straightening the curl. When she released it, the tendril coiled back like a watch spring.

"Please do." He headed for the steps before he gave in to the temptation to see if he could make her hair spring back from his fingers, too. "I'd rather not have that mane end up in my soup."

Behind him, the front door closed with a bit more force than necessary. When he glanced over the railing, only a spark of carroty hair flashed by on the way to the kitchen and back steps. That door closed more gently than the street entrance, and Gordon stood alone at the head of the staircase.

The cavernous foyer yawned below him, rising two stories so that the fanlight window above the door spread out across from him, and a skylight glowed red and blue and green above him. The upstairs hallway stretched out like a road he knew would lead him away from where he wanted to be—east toward the sea, not west toward another ocean, snow, ice, gold.

Jaw tense, he stalked down the hallway to where his bedroom overlooked the back garden and the house next door. He could see the ocean from the back windows, too, the capricious, stormy Atlantic. How he'd wanted to sail on that ocean, lift the canvas to the wind and disappear without the noise and stench of the steam engines. He liked sails with their peace and struggle of man against nature, or man working with nature. He'd objected when their father began to get rid of the sailboats for their excursion company and replace them with the steam-powered vessels. Father had kept one sailboat until Gordon—

He slammed the door on that memory and opened his bedroom door. As Ruby had claimed, nothing had changed. Framed watercolors and photographs of sailboats lined the walls. Blue and white curtains fluttered at the open windows, wafting the scent of the sea around the spotlessly clean chamber. His model ships still graced the mantel, bedside table, and every other available surface.

"Welcome home," he said with a sardonic twist to his lips, setting his valise on the floor with a thud.

He opened the door that had been the dressing room he and his brother had shared, curious to know if his clothes had been kept, too. They hadn't. The large closet was indeed a bathroom now, complete with basin and tub. If the aroma of roast beef and tarts hadn't been climbing the back stairs to creep under his door, he would have taken advantage of the latter. Every muscle ached from days on the train. His stomach hurt worse, gnawing at his insides in demand of food.

He settled for a wash and change of shirt and necktie, a comb through his hair, and a touch of water to hold it in place off his face. Then he descended the steps, finding Beryl and Ruby perched side by side on the sofa, as though awaiting a photograph portrait to be taken—or sentencing.

He was going to sentence them.

Shaking off that ridiculous thought, he offered them a smile and held out his arms. "May I escort you lovely ladies to dinner?"

"It's more proper for you to escort Miss Marigold," Beryl said. "Since she's so old."

Gordon lowered his arms. "Miss McCorkle eats with us?"

"Of course." Ruby spoke around her fingers. "We're too little to eat alone."

"You're too little to eat alone." Beryl stuck her nose in the air. "I am quite capable of taking care of myself."

"But when your parents were—here. . ." Gordon glanced toward the patter of footfalls in the hallway, a click of heels.

"We ate in the nursery." Beryl narrowed her eyes at him. "Don't you know anything about children?"

"Apparently no more than you know of manners, Miss Beryl." Marigold strode into the room, her hair already beginning to slip from the knot on the back of her neck. "You know better than to talk to an adult that way. Now, apologize."

The girl's blue eyes clashed with the woman's green ones. Gordon expected to see sparks ignite in the middle. Beryl's mouth thinned. Marigold's grew thinner.

And Ruby began to cry. "Just say you're sorry, Beryl. I don't want Uncle Gordon to go away like Mommy and Daddy."

No sparks ignited from the older two females, but the younger one's words sent an arrow straight into Gordon's heart.

Apparently it struck Beryl, too, for she bowed her head. "I'm sorry," she mumbled.

"It's—" Gordon found his chest too tight for easy speech. "I accept your apology, Beryl. I should have realized you wouldn't normally eat in the dining room."

"And speaking of eating," Marigold said, "Mrs. Cromwell is waiting for us."

He wouldn't ask her why she wasn't helping the house-keeper serve. He'd already stepped into deep waters in this familiar yet unfamiliar household. Nor did he offer Marigold his arm. He simply stood back and gestured for the ladies to go ahead of him into the dining room.

It, too, had remained much the same, with the long french windows open to the verandah, filmy draperies floating on the sea breeze, and silver shining in the late afternoon sunshine. White linen gleamed like new snow. The chairs remained the heavy mahogany from his parents' day, but now the cushions were deep blue instead of red. Likewise, the velvet hangings on either side of the windows had been changed to blue.

Mrs. Cromwell trotted in from the kitchen, bearing a laden tray; she had changed more than anything he'd seen thus far. Her hair held far more silver than black, and her eyes reflected the milky cast of cataracts. Her shoulders stooped, and the food dishes appeared to weigh more than she did.

"My dear Mrs. Cromwell." Gordon stepped toward the woman who had sneaked him cookies when he was a lad, who had added an apple to his supper of bread and water when he'd been sent to his room without supper. "Mrs. Cromwell," he repeated, for lack of anything better coming to his lips.

Marigold turned from tucking a napkin into the neckline of Ruby's dress and stepped between Gordon and Mrs. Cromwell. "Let me take that." She removed the tray from the old lady's gnarled hands. "I'll make sure everyone gets everything, but go hug Mr. Chambers, as I know you're anxious to do."

"Hug him?" Mrs. Cromwell fixed her brown eyes on Gordon. He wanted to squirm.

"I suppose all those apples I sent up to you spoiled you so much you forgot your duty to your family." She scowled. "What took you so long to get here?"

"Too many things to say without spoiling dinner." Gordon held out his arms.

Mrs. Cromwell embraced him, then swung away, dabbing her apron to the corners of her eyes. "Come into the kitchen after dinner and tell me."

She beat a hasty retreat.

Gordon returned to the table and his wide-eyed nieces. "I thought she was old when I was your age."

"She's at least seventy-five now," Marigold said from where she dished up plates of food at the sideboard. "She wants to retire to Georgia with her sister."

"I can arrange for that." Gordon picked up his glass of

lemonade and sipped. He hadn't tasted many lemons in his wanderings of the past eleven years. The sweet tartness triggered a hundred memories of picnics on the beach or aboard one of the boats.

"She can't go away," Ruby protested. "Who will cook for us?"

"He'll hire someone else." Beryl frowned at the plate Marigold slid before her. "I expect he'll hire lots of new servants now."

"I hope he doesn't expect me to cook." Marigold laughed, as she set food before Ruby and him. "We'd be eating eggs and bread for every meal."

The girls made faces.

Gordon dropped his gaze to his plate. With each passing moment, his plan to leave seemed more and more difficult. But not impossible. He would have to find the girls a school quickly. A boarding school, perhaps in Philadelphia, some place where they could remain on holidays, too, or find friends who would take them home.

"Will you ask the blessing, sir?" Marigold asked. "Before the food gets cold?"

"Of course." Gordon reached out a hand to each of his nieces. Two hands, less than half the size of his, tucked themselves into his palms like trusting kittens. For a moment, he couldn't speak, couldn't think of anything but these small charges, couldn't recall what one said in a blessing. No one in mining camps or aboard freighters asked the blessing over a meal. The silence grew, profound enough for the drone of bees outside the window to sound like distant engines and his stomach rumbling to resemble thunder.

"Thank You for Mr. Chambers' safe arrival," Miss Marigold murmured from the other side of Ruby.

"Yes." Gordon cleared his throat. "Thank You for a good journey and for the health of these children. Thank You for this meal we are about to partake and for the hands that prepared it. Amen."

"Amen." Beryl removed her hand from his.

"Thank You for the blackberry tarts." Ruby added her own blessing.

"You have to eat your green beans first," Beryl admonished.

"I will." Ruby picked up her fork and stabbed a mouthful of beans.

Smiling, Gordon tucked into the food himself. While the first savory bite of roast beef fairly melted on his tongue, he conjured questions he could ask the girls. He should get to know them, his last living relations.

Or maybe he shouldn't. If he was leaving in a week or two, why should he allow himself to get close to them?

He continued to eat in silence.

"Girls, tell your uncle what we've been reading." Marigold McCorkle wasn't eating. She perched on her chair, a forkful of potatoes balanced in her hand, and darted glances between Gordon and his nieces. "Tell him about reading *Little Women*."

"Beth didn't come back." Ruby's face screwed up. "Jo shouldn't have cut off her hair. Maybe Beth would have come back if she hadn't cut her hair."

"She couldn't come back," Beryl said with a twist of her lips. "She's dead like—"

"Beryl." Marigold's voice cut through Beryl's scornful response to her sister, though the nurserymaid never spoke above a murmur.

"Beth was sick," Beryl said in a gentler tone. "That's why she didn't come back."

"Mommy and Daddy weren't sick." Ruby smiled for the first time since Gordon's arrival. " 'Cause drowning isn't the same as being sick."

"No, it's not." Gordon looked to Marigold for help before he said more.

She caressed Ruby's cheek. "No, my dear, it's not the same. But your mother and father. . . Here, eat these lovely tomatoes. They're fresh out of the garden."

As delicious as the food was, Gordon had lost his appetite. He finished what remained on his plate, while allowing

Marigold to direct the conversation around walks on the boardwalk, the pretty shells they'd found on the beach, the dolphins they'd spied from the lighthouse.

"And the nel—the. . .elephant!" Ruby cried. "I want to go inside the elephant."

"The elephant." Gordon laughed suddenly. "I remember drinking sodas at the top—"

"It's not safe now," Marigold cut in with such sharpness he jerked back in his chair.

"That's too bad." Gordon set his knife and fork on his plate in an *X*, rearranged them into a cross, then returned them to an *X*, watching Miss Marigold all the time. "What else has changed?"

"I wouldn't know." She held his gaze. "I've only lived here since a year ago May."

"May I be excused?" Beryl folded her napkin next to her plate. "I want to go read the next part of 'A Little Princess.'"

"Of course," Gordon said at the same time Marigold said, "Not until Ruby is finished eating."

"Those magazines with 'A Little Princess' in them have been around for over ten years," Marigold continued. "They can wait for another fifteen minutes."

"I want my blackberry tart." Ruby made a face and shoved the last green bean into her mouth.

Memory flashed into Gordon's head. Him as a boy, probably her age, aching for dessert, hating the vegetables on his plate. Both had become precious to him during his wanderings.

"You don't want your sweet?" he asked Beryl.

"No thank you." Beryl stood. "I don't like berries."

"Beryl, sit down," Marigold commanded.

"Uncle Gordon said I could leave." With that pronouncement, the girl stomped from the room.

Ruby's lower lip quivered. "Oh no, she's being naughty. Bad things happen to naughty girls."

"No, no they don't." Marigold slipped her arm around the child. "Why would you think that?"

"Why indeed?" Gordon scowled at the governess. "And Beryl isn't being naughty. I told her she could be excused. Now cheer up, or Mrs. Cromwell will think you don't like her cooking."

Ruby, however, looked pale and tense. She slipped out from under Marigold's arm and mumbled a request to be excused. "I need to be with Beryl."

"All right." Marigold looked pained.

Gordon stood. "I'll get the door for you." He opened the heavy panel, waited for Ruby to head up the stairs, then turned back to the nurserymaid. "You're right, Miss McCorkle. This upset to Ruby is a fine example why one of us has to be the authority around here, and, as their guardian, that is me."

"When you know nothing about them?" Marigold stood, her hands on her hips, her hair fanning out around her head like a lion's mane. "When I have risked my future happiness for them, you want me to step aside and tell them to listen to you and not me?"

"I haven't seen that you do such a fine job of it, madam." Gordon clasped his hands behind his back. "Beryl is insolent, and Ruby is anxious and seems to think her parents will come back. That looks like poor guidance to me."

"Poor guidance, Mr. Chambers, is leaving us in limbo for three months and making me stay here for three months longer than I ne—eeded to."

To his horror, her voice broke, her eyes sparkled extra bright, and her lower lip quivered.

He set his jaw against the lure of feminine tears. "If you should have left three months ago, madam, then don't let me keep you here. There's still enough daylight left for you to pack and reach your destination before dark."

three

Marigold clapped her hands to her head, flattening out her hair as best she could. As though that would hold in the tidal wave of outrage surging up her throat like bile.

"Mr. Chambers," she said with exaggerated calm, "I would love to leave. I wanted to leave three months ago. I was planning on leaving the day after Ruby's birthday, but your brother and sister-in-law were killed, you didn't respond to the telegrams for weeks, and I wouldn't abandon the girls any more then than I will now, to see them dropped into a school and left thinking no one loves them."

"That won't happen for several weeks, perhaps months." Gordon Chambers began to pace along a line of roses woven into the carpet. "I will have to sell the business and get my brother's financial affairs in order. Selling the business this time of year may be difficult." He completed a circuit and began the walk again. "I'll have to speak with the lawyer. I'll have to find an appropriate school." He reached the far end of the room and faced Marigold, his eyes as cold as deep brown could be. "But I won't keep you here."

"You can't take care of the girls on your own. It'll take time to find an appropriate governess or nurserymaid, even if you can find one who is willing to work for only a month or two."

"Mrs. Cromwell—"

"Cannot take care of the house and oversee the girls' education and care," Marigold cut in.

Gordon narrowed his eyes. "Do you have no respect for others, Miss McCorkle?"

"Of course." He was going to dismiss her anyway, so she added, "When the person deserves it."

"I see." He crossed his arms over his broad chest and clamped his lips together, but one corner twitched suspiciously.

Marigold flung out her hands, sending what pins remained cascading onto the floor and her curls bounding about her head like corks on waves. "Mrs. Cromwell has already told me she will leave within a month of your arrival. She wants out of this climate before winter comes."

"Are you willing to stay until arrangements can be made?" Gordon asked.

"I'm willing, but I can't."

"Because you've decided to dislike me even before I arrived?"

"No, because I can't remain in this house alone without a respectable woman like Mrs. Cromwell here to lend propriety to the arrangement."

"Of course. I should have thought of that." A faint flush rose along his high cheekbones. "Then what do you suggest I do?"

"Stay, Mr. Chambers. Your nieces need you."

"I know nothing about children. I've lived aboard ships or in mining camps since I was eighteen years old."

"You can learn." Marigold's heart ached. Her passion for seeing their futures as secure as two orphaned girls' lives could be, she pressed on. "You can keep the business in the family for them to have a heritage, keep this house so they have something familiar on school holidays, give them Christmas and summers here, as they've always had." Her voice broke. "Give them as much of a family as possible so their lives aren't wholly empty of love."

"But I can't carry on my own life, make my own business and future, if I stay here, not that that's any of your business."

"No, sir, it's not." Marigold clenched her hands at her sides to stop herself from throwing something across the room—preferably at his head. God wouldn't honor such behavior. Nor would He want her to spew out the words blazing on her tongue. God would want her to—what?

Grovel so Gordon Chambers wouldn't send her away and make the girls lose one more person solid and secure in their lives?

She gritted her teeth until her jaw ached. Her chin felt like carved marble. She could barely open her lips to speak. "Mr. Chambers, if you can find a respectable woman to take Mrs. Cromwell's place, I will guard my tongue about my opinions and see to the girls' welfare until"—every word felt like she was having to expel a cannonball—"until you can make arrangements for them."

"That must have cost you a year's worth of your pride, Miss McCorkle." He grinned.

She flinched away from its charm and melting impact on her senses. And she kept silent.

"If I don't agree to your terms," Gordon continued, "do you have somewhere to go?"

"Yes, sir, I do."

More than the girls had—a family, a sister getting married, an opportunity to mend the breach with Lucian, her supposed fiancé—if that were possible.

"Mrs. Cromwell wants to leave in a month?" Gordon persisted.

Marigold nodded. "Yes, that's when her sister leaves for Georgia. If she goes later, she'll have to travel all that way alone."

"Then that gives me four weeks to work things out, doesn't it?" He shoved his fingers into his thick, wavy dark hair. "Let us put our spat behind us and declare a truce, all right?"

"For the sake of the girls, yes." Marigold held out her hand to shake but couldn't help adding, "It gives me four weeks to make you see that abandoning the children is not a good decision."

He laughed out loud, a rich rumbling exclamation of mirth. Then he strode forward and clasped Marigold's hand with his warm, strong fingers.

She started as though she'd touched a live electrical wire.

He snatched his hand away and rubbed it on the skirt of his coat. Without another word, he turned on his heel and stalked from the room.

Marigold perched on the edge of the nearest chair and stared out the window. She didn't know how she could like a thing about him, not his eyes, not his smile, and definitely not his touch. She should scrub her hand—erase the sensation of his strength, the kind of strength of a man who could pull a lady from danger and hold her in safety and security.

A lady? Didn't she mean two little girls who desperately needed a permanent home, something to depend on in a world that had gone topsy-turvy for them in a single clap of thunder and stroke of lightning?

Of course she did. She was merely tired and overwrought and thoroughly determined that nothing less than Gordon Chambers remaining in Cape May would satisfy her. Nothing else was the right decision. She would make him stay if she had to—had to. . .

She'd think of something.

Meanwhile, she had promised to help Mrs. Cromwell with the cleaning up so she could talk to Gordon Chambers herself. Then the girls would want a story before bedtime. Ruby would want her to hold hands until she slept. . . .

Feeling like the rag with which she was about to do dishes, Marigold stumbled into the kitchen. Mrs. Cromwell had put the extra food away, but pots, pans, and dishes littered the worktable. Through the open back door, Marigold caught a glimpse of the housekeeper talking with Gordon on the porch. They held glasses of lemonade, and a plate of ginger cookies rested on a table between them. Their voices carried into the house. Though the words remained indistinct, the tone spoke of affection, kindness, and sorrow.

Marigold rested one hand on the edge of the sink and closed her eyes. "God, please forgive me. I am still too selfish and wanting things the way I want them."

No sense of peace washed through her. She knew God

didn't approve of her stiff-necked pride, her certainty that she knew what was best for everyone. Yet she couldn't help herself. Other people just made a mess of their lives. Mr. and Mrs. Chambers shouldn't have gone out in the boat that late May afternoon. Marigold had told them of the weather, had predicted a storm. She felt storms coming in the place where she'd broken her arm as a child.

Or rather, when one of the Grassick boys had pushed her out of a tree.

Thoughts of her childhood friends made her smile. They were scattered around the country now like she and her own siblings—attending college and work, military service, and positions at the Grassick Glassworks.

The glassworks, where she should be living with her husband, one of the glassblowers, and proudly displaying her inheritance passed down from a Grassick to her family nearly half a century earlier—the goldfinch bottle, the symbol of love, loyalty, constancy, and hope that had resided in her bedchamber at home since she and Lucian announced their engagement nearly a year and a half ago.

A lifetime ago.

She picked up a sturdy skillet and slammed it into the sink. Scrubbing away the remnants of food might help alleviate her annoyance at the man outside, whose rumbling laughter drifted in through the open door.

"That's right. Enjoy your homecoming that has cost me so much." She gritted her teeth to stop herself from growling like the kitten.

Suds lathering up her arms, she made herself sing, running through her favorite hymns. It helped keep her from dwelling on her anger with Gordon Chambers and pass the time through the onerous work of cleaning the kitchen.

"Hark! The herald angels sing—"

The rumbling laughter broke through Marigold's recital with such a blow she gasped, choked, and coughed.

"I didn't mean to scare you." Gordon Chambers touched

her shoulder. "I wanted to find out who has the angelic voice in here."

"Angelic you think?" She set her soapy hands on her hips and frowned at him. "Are you in the habit of laughing at things you consider angelic?"

"No, ma'am." He backed off as though frightened. "I was merely amused to hear Christmas carols in August."

"Christmas—oh." Her cheeks heated from more than the steaming water. "I was just singing the songs I can remember without the words in front of me."

"Please, don't let me stop you. I merely returned for more lemonade." He glanced at the icebox. "Where are the girls?"

"Playing in the schoolroom, from the sound of it." Marigold glanced upward, where a series of light thumps, creaks, and an occasional giggle drifted through the floorboards. "They're quite good about that, playing on their own, that is."

"Should I—um—take them some refreshment?"

"That's very thoughtful of you." Marigold dropped the last plate into the dishwater. "But I'll get them a snack when I'm done here. They'll be ready for bed by then."

When he neither moved nor spoke, she looked at him again, eyebrows raised.

"It's still light out. Isn't that too early for bed?" he asked.

"Not when you're six and nine."

"I didn't know." He swung toward the icebox. "How do we get more ice? This chunk looks nearly done."

"He comes by in the mornings and leaves it for us." She couldn't resist adding, "And I'm sure he'd like to be paid."

"As would you, I imagine."

"It won't go amiss," she hedged.

She didn't need the meager wages of a nurserymaid, but he didn't need to know that. In fact, she'd rather he didn't know that her family was probably as well-off or more so than the Chamberses. If he did, he'd ask too many questions. Marigold didn't want to answer questions about herself.

"I'll visit the bank tomorrow," Gordon said.

"Grand." Marigold lifted her now-red hands from the dishwater. "I'll see to the girls. If you wish to say good night to them, please do so."

"I'll think about it." He retrieved the pitcher of lemonade from the icebox and retreated to the porch.

He didn't come up to wish the girls good night. Though Marigold read them a second story, much to Ruby's delight, she heard no sound of footfalls on the steps leading to the top floor and nursery.

"I told you he doesn't want us," Beryl pronounced in the middle of *Cinderella*.

"He's probably weary from his journey." Although she was no doubt telling the truth of this, Marigold felt like a liar making excuses for the girls' unfeeling uncle.

In her own room, adjacent to the one the girls shared, she sank onto her knees and tried to pray for an extra helping of grace. A half hour later, cramped from remaining in the same position, she rose and readied herself for sleep. She knew God possessed it but wasn't certain He would give her the amount of forgiveness needed to cover Gordon Chambers.

four

Gordon escaped from the house at what he hoped was an early enough hour to avoid sharing breakfast with his nieces and their nursemaid, especially the nursemaid. No one had made him feel guilty with a look since the last time he'd seen his father. And the last thing he wanted right now was a reminder of the parent who had driven him from the house and ensured Gordon wouldn't want to return.

None of them, apparently, had planned on Gordon needing to return.

But there he was, striding along the quiet street and headed toward the sea. Sunlight spilled through the branches of the trees, and a cool breeze off the sea stirred air that would later become oppressively hot and humid except near the water. The aromas of hot dog and sweetmeat vendors didn't yet invade the fresh air along the boardwalk. With the tide coming in, only the sea itself scented the morning.

Gordon paused at the edge of the sand and gazed toward the rising sun. As yet uninhabited by too many people in bathing costumes or women in hats so wide they surely limited the wearer's sight, the beach formed the perfect view for a postcard. Gordon wished he owned a camera so he could capture this moment. It would better serve his memories of this place he should think of as home than the stormy winter day and voices shouting louder than thunder that plagued his dreams.

"Life here wasn't all strife and sorrow," he told a passing flock of seagulls.

They screeched at him, as though condemning him for not tossing them any bread.

"I'll remember tomorrow," he promised.

A pity his life had been full of promises he intended to carry out tomorrow. Tomorrow he would make a fortune on his own. Tomorrow he would return and show that fortune to his brother to prove he wasn't a ne'er-do-well. Tomorrow he would remedy the financial problems plaguing his nieces and their household.

He set his jaw. "Today, I'll go to the bank. No, I'll go to the boathouse."

The latter was closer. There, from a neat, whitewashed building set at the end of a pier near Second Street, visitors to Cape May had been able to take excursions around the cape and into Delaware Bay for thirty years. Gordon's father had started the business when he grew weary of being a naval captain during the Civil War and then a merchantman captain. He'd made a lot of money doing both and found the peaceful seaside town of Cape May perfect for his young family and business dedicated to bringing people enjoyment in one of God's greatest creations—the ocean. The early boats had all been sailing vessels. By the time Gordon left home, all were powered by steam, noisier, but able to go regardless of the winds and with fewer crew members.

As a boy, Gordon loved watching the dolphins in the bay and the occasional pods of whales. Now the temptation to take out one of the craft bobbing at anchor and keep sailing until he could see neither land nor mankind quickened his pace. The realization that no one would yet be at work slowed it again.

"That should change," he mused aloud. "If sightseers could view the sunrise from the sea—"

He cut himself off. His father had severed him from the business because of one youthful prank, and if the old man hadn't wanted his younger son involved, then Gordon would sell it. Two little girls couldn't manage things. They would need a trusted manager for that.

As they'd needed for the past three months.

Gordon paused to gaze into the rising sun again, in an

attempt to recapture his earlier peace. But others now invaded the quiet early morning. A man with a camera set upon a tripod perched at the edge of the tide line. Three elderly ladies in straw bonnets dug about in the sand with sticks. Seeking treasure or pretty shells?

Gordon started to smile at the memory of how the smallest find felt like the discovery of Blackbeard's gold. He raised a hand and opened his mouth to wish the ladies good luck.

"Uncle Gordon! Uncle Gordon!" The chorus of childish voices rang on the breeze. "Uncle, wait!"

Not waiting would be churlish. Plastering a smile on his face, Gordon faced his nieces and their governess.

The girls wore identical white dresses with black ribbon trim, a concession to their mourning. Ribbons fluttered from their white straw hats, and they carried miniature parasols with ruffled edges. With their golden curls and blue eyes, they could pose in front of the ocean for the photographer and make his picture perfect.

Miss Marigold was another matter. Her gray frock bore not a bit of trimming. If not for her vivid hair beneath a plain hat, she would have blended into the weathered boards upon which she strode. But the hair, as he was growing accustomed to seeing, sprang out behind her as though it wanted to go in different directions than the head to which the curls were attached.

And so did he. Though his lips twitched into a reluctant smile—or perhaps because of the urge to grin, even laugh at Marigold McCorkle—Gordon wanted to head in another direction than one that would bring him into greater proximity with the uppity woman.

"You're out early," he greeted them instead. "It's a wonder you had time for breakfast."

"She always makes us eat breakfast." Ruby stuck her fingers in her mouth.

Gordon reached out his hand and tugged them free. "I thought only babies sucked on their fingers."

"She is a baby." Beryl tossed her head. Her hat ribbons fluttered like small birds. "She started doing that after Mommy and Daddy. . ." Her lower lip quivered before she finished her sentence. Hauteur left her face.

"They went away." Ruby stared at her fingers, still resting in Gordon's hand. "Mommy promised me a new doll last time I stopped sucking my fingers. Do you think"—she glanced from Gordon to Marigold, her eyes sparkling—"if I stop this time Mommy and Daddy will come home?"

"They can't." Beryl's voice was flat.

Gordon's heart felt flattened.

Marigold yanked a handkerchief from her pocketbook and dabbed at the corners of her pretty green eyes. "I'm sorry, Ruby, sweetheart." She coughed. "Your mommy and daddy went to heaven and can't come back. Remember what the pastor said?"

"Yes." Ruby nodded, started to stick her fingers into her mouth again, then curled her tiny hand around Gordon's fingers instead. "Will you go for our walk with us?"

"We can return if we're disturbing you, Mr. Chambers," Marigold said. "I didn't realize—we like to come out early before it's too crowded and hot down here."

"My own thoughts." As much as he wanted to tell them he was heading to the boathouse, where he doubted they'd be welcome, Gordon shrugged. "It's a public walkway. If you wish to keep going, I won't stop you."

Not exactly gracious.

His conscience stinging him, and Ruby's small hand in his, prompted him to add, "Of course I'll join you."

"Thank you." Ruby tugged on his hand and started skipping down the walkway.

Marigold didn't hold her back. "That's thoughtful of you." She flashed him a smile warm enough to make the August sun feel inadequate.

Beryl said nothing, but her solemn little face brightened as she trotted along, twirling her parasol.

"We're going to look for dolphins," Ruby announced. "I saw one the day Mommy and Daddy went away and wondered why he didn't find them. Miss Marigold says dolphins are intell–intell—" She ended on a sigh.

"Intelligent?" Gordon suggested.

"Yes, it means smart." Ruby grinned up at him, showing that she was missing one of her incisors.

Suddenly, Gordon remembered losing one of his own teeth around her age.

"Did you put that tooth under your pillow when you lost it?" he asked.

"I did." Ruby changed from a skip to a hop. The heels of her shoes clattered on the walk. "And I got a penny there instead the next day."

"She's getting rich." Marigold laughed. "Three pennies since April."

"I got a whole dime once." Gordon gazed into the distance, a distance beyond the visible world around them. "It was just what I needed to buy the sails for my model ship."

All three females stopped to gaze at him as though he'd grown two heads or sprouted wings.

"You made all those model ships?" Marigold asked.

"I haven't always been a grumpy old man." He feigned indignation.

The little girls giggled.

The grown-up lady colored something akin to her hair. "I only meant—I thought they were given to you. They're so. . . good."

"I've always loved the sea."

"But you were in New Mexico." Miss Marigold still looked bewildered. "There's no sea there."

"I've been to sea. I've been on land." He shrugged. "Wherever my fortunes or misfortunes have taken me."

"Do you have a fortune?" Ruby asked. "Or a misfortune?"

"Ruby, I don't think that's a polite question." Miss Marigold took Ruby's hand in hers. "We should be going home and not asking your uncle impertinent questions."

"If he had a fortune," Beryl spoke up, "he wouldn't want to be going off to Alaska for gold."

"How did you know—" Gordon caught himself too late.

He had all the females' undivided attention once again and felt his own face heating from more than the early sunshine could be causing.

"I heard him talking to Mrs. Cromwell last evening." Beryl twirled her parasol in everyone's faces before tilting it back over her shoulder. "The nursery windows are right over the back porch, you know."

"I'd forgotten." Gordon thinned his lips. "I'll have to find a better place to talk in the future."

"We heard the gardener kissing one of the maids there," Ruby announced. "So don't kiss anyone there, either."

"All right." Marigold, though blushing, barely managed to suppress her laughter. "We need to get to your lessons."

"But you said we can go to the lighthouse," Beryl protested.

Gordon glanced down to the point of land jutting out between the Atlantic and the entrance to Delaware Bay. A lighthouse soared into the sky, its lamp appearing darkened in the daylight but ready to glow as soon as dusk fell to warn ships away from the cape or lead them toward the safety of the bay and harbor.

"It won't be open for visitors now," Gordon murmured. "Maybe later. . ."

He'd loved that lighthouse as a boy, all the way up to the day he left. Since then, he'd seen dozens more around the world, taller, fancier lighthouses. None had said home—

He slammed the door on that memory, too.

"I need to get down to the boathouse." His tone was deliberately brusque. "I expect someone will be there soon."

"The first excursion starts at eight o'clock," Beryl informed him. "That's in another forty-five minutes, so someone had better be there."

"We haven't been since the accident." Marigold sidled

closer to him to speak in an undertone. "Maybe you can take the girls out on one of the boats so they don't become afraid of the water. It would be a pity for the owners of a boating company to fear water."

"But they won't be—" Gordon glanced at the children, realized that little ones did have big ears, and nodded. "We'll see what happens during my visit."

"Your visit?" Ruby snatched at his hand again. "I thought you were here to live."

"I can't—" He gazed into her guileless blue eyes, and what he couldn't do was say he was leaving as soon as he could.

In that moment, he understood why Marigold McCorkle had stayed behind, even when she wanted to leave. Abandoning these children would be downright cruel, if a body let them grow fond of him. Or if he grew fond of them.

"He has to find gold." Beryl engendered the last word with scorn, as though it were a foul substance.

"Beryl," Marigold spoke with gentle firmness, "remember what Proverbs says about mockers."

"I wasn't—" Beryl sighed. "I'm sorry. I guess we should go home now. It's getting hot."

It wasn't, but her pale cheeks had turned scarlet.

"I'll see the three of you at lunch." Gordon offered them a bow.

The girls dropped curtsies then gave Marigold their hands and headed back toward the residential part of town.

Gordon watched the trio until a growing crowd of people swallowed them up in a froth of pale gowns and fussy parasols. Even then, he didn't move until someone bumped him and apologized profusely.

"All this camera equipment—" The photographer from the beach turned pale. "Gerald, I thought you were—that is. . ."

"I'm Gordon Chambers." Gordon's shoulders stiffened. "Gerald's brother."

The man laughed, and his color returned to normal. "Cole Ambrose, local photographer and friend of your brother. I'd shake your hand if mine weren't so full."

Gordon shifted from one foot to the other. "Wayfarer and black sheep of the family."

Ambrose laughed, a rich "Haw-haw" that boomed across the sand like breakers. "Never heard your brother say that about you—the black sheep part. All Gerald ever said was you liked to wander and had seen most of the world."

"I don't think 'most' is accurate." Gordon smelled smoke and wondered if it was coming from the boat engines firing up. The rumble of powerful motors told him he was right and gave him a good excuse to extricate himself from the stranger's clutches.

Except he felt oddly reluctant to do so. This man, with his broad smile and bright hazel eyes, demonstrated such warmth, leaving him standing on the boardwalk with his arms full of camera equipment would have been worse than rude.

And Gordon wanted to know more of what his brother hadn't said against him.

"I have seen a good part of the world, though," Gordon added.

"Oh, I want to do that, take pictures of lions in Africa and elephants in India." Ambrose laughed. "But the Lord's seen fit to keep me here taking pictures of sunrises in New Jersey."

"There was an elephant here once, wasn't there?" Gordon scanned the horizon and found the joy of his youth, a wood and tin elephant, rising seventy feet in the distance.

Ambrose grimaced. "It's an eyesore now and is scheduled to be demolished any day. No one could make money off of that monstrosity. But I got pictures of it in its glory days. And pictures from the top of it. What a pleasure. Happy to show them to you. Stop by my studio anytime."

"Thank you. I just might do that." That was the polite thing to say, yet Gordon thought he just might.

The girls would enjoy—

No, he mustn't take them on outings. They might grow to

care for him, and he. . .

Already cared for them. How could he not? Ruby, so young and needing of attention and reassurance; Beryl, trying to be older than she was and so haughty. Marigold. . .

"Can you manage all that equipment all the way back to town?" Gordon found himself asking.

"Do it all the time. My wife says it keeps me from getting fat from her cooking." Ambrose nodded as though reaching a conclusion. "Now that you're here, we'll have you over for dinner."

"I won't be here for long," Gordon admitted.

A flash of disappointment crossed Ambrose's face. "Then we'll make it sooner than later. Have a blessed day."

His stride jaunty despite his heavy equipment, he trotted toward town.

Gordon watched him for a few moments; then, feeling as though his morning had been spent seeing others walk away from him, he spun on his heel and marched to the boathouse.

Two of the small steam-powered boats bobbed and smoked along the dock. A couple dozen people in hats and carrying hampers of food stood in line, where two pretty young women in garb resembling sailor costumes with skirts instead of trousers stood taking tickets.

Gordon nodded to them then entered the office.

The instant he opened the door, the smell of paper and ink overwhelmed the odors of smoke and sea. Dust motes danced in shafts of sunlight streaming through windows that could stand to be washed, and piles of ledgers covered every surface.

Behind these piles, two clerks bent over open account books and a third counted money at a till.

The money man glanced up. "Tickets are sold out—" Like Cole Ambrose, the man paled.

"Gordon Chambers," he said with haste. "Mr. Gerald Chambers' brother and now his daughters' guardian."

Much to his bewilderment still.

"Of course. Of course." The man nodded like a marionette with a broken string. "The resemblance. . . Well, sir, it's extraordinary."

"Of course it is." Gordon managed a stiff-lipped smile. "We were twins."

"I see. I see." The man glanced toward each of the clerks, who stared openly at Gordon. "You'll be wanting to talk to Mr. Randall. He's the manager."

"Yes, I would. Is he in?"

"He is. He is."

Without being told, one of the as-yet-silent clerks scrambled off his stool and retreated to the back of the office and knocked on a door. A high, thin voice commanded him to enter. Moments later, he emerged and beckoned Gordon forward. "Mr. Randall will see you, sir."

Gordon wound his way between tall desks and overflowing shelves until he reached the rear office. A reedy man stood behind a massive desk nearly bare of papers and books—but not of dust.

Didn't they ever clean?

Gordon stifled a sneeze and held out his hand. "Gordon Chambers."

"Lawrence Randall. So pleased you could finally join us." Randall shook Gordon's hand. "Dockerty, fetch us some coffee."

The clerk departed. Courtesies were exchanged as to the weather and journeys and the wellness of one another's families. Then the coffee arrived, rich and piping hot, and the two men got to work.

"Do you know anything about accounting ledgers?" Randall asked.

"I was the supercargo on a merchantman for two years."

"That'll do."

They bent their heads over the latest figures, the busiest summer months and the months since Gerald's death. Gordon added figures in his head, as he'd always done, and found the accounting of receipts and expenditures meticulously recorded.

"It appears you've done well by the business," Gordon said after two hours of too much coffee and too many numbers. "I appreciate your time." He rose. "In a few days, I'd like to go out on a couple of the boats, if that's possible."

"Of course we'll make room for you, sir." Randall shook Gordon's hand in farewell. "We're full-up about a week in advance, so you'll have to wait and see if someone doesn't show up or cancels. Don't like to overcrowd the boats, you know."

"I do know. Send word if you have a cancellation. And I'll be taking the girls and their governess out on the water as soon as you have openings for four."

"We'll try." Randall's long, narrow face grew even longer. "Mr. Chambers never took his family aboard the public excursion boats, since they had the family one. But that's gone." He sighed. "We all told him not to go out that day, but he saw that pod of dolphins and wanted to show his wife."

"Interesting." Gordon had never known his brother, older by thirty minutes, to be impulsive like that. "A tragic mistake."

Wanting no more talk of Gerald, he beat a hasty retreat and headed back along the boardwalk at a brisk pace—or tried to. He hadn't gone more than a dozen feet before an older gentleman in clean but ragged clothes stepped in front of him, barring his path.

"Are you Gordon Chambers?" the man asked.

"I am." Gordon frowned. "What do you—"

"Dennis Tripp." The gentleman held out his hand.

Gordon didn't take it. "How may I help you?"

"It's not how you may help me, sir," Tripp announced, "it's how I may help you."

"Oh?" Gordon glanced from side to side, deciding which way to take to evade the man.

Tripp caught hold of his arm. "You've got to listen to me, sir." He spoke in a whispering rush.

"Why?" Gordon removed the hand with gentle firmness.

He'd met such men all over the world, those not quite right in their heads, wanting to predict doom and gloom and the end of the world. Most of them wanted money. Gordon had brought none of the latter with him.

"You want to save lives," Tripp said. "And you won't—"

"Good day, Mr. Tripp." Gordon skirted the man and continued walking.

Tripp fell into step beside him. "I'm not a madman, Mr. Chambers. I'm telling you the truth. If you listen to Lawrence Randall about how well the business is doing, people will die on one of those boats one of these days."

Gordon skidded to a halt and glared at the man. "I'd be careful about spouting that kind of nonsense, Mr. Tripp. If you drive business away, you can expect serious legal trouble."

"It's worth the risk." Tripp clasped his hands before him as though he were praying. "I worked for the Chambers Excursion and Sailing Company until a month ago. When I discovered Randall and his minions were dishonest and confronted him, he dismissed me."

A disgruntled employee.

With a sigh, Gordon stopped. "All right, let's have this out here and now. Randall dismissed you, so you want to get even with him."

"No, sir. He's a nice man and a fair manager." Tripp's gray eyes looked straight into Gordon's. "But he's dishonest, sir. He shows expenses for boats being repaired, but there haven't been any repairs made on those boats all season."

five

Marigold decided to let Gordon see to the girls' dinner. Though he'd tried to hide it, she'd noticed the softening of his hard features in response to Ruby's eagerness and Beryl's condescension. He had even smiled once or twice, and little gold lights, rather like trapped sunbeams, had danced in his eyes. If the girls won him over, perhaps he wouldn't leave.

"And you can?" She scowled at her reflection in a silver bowl that stood on the foyer table.

When the Chamberses had been alive, that bowl overflowed with invitations to dinners and picnics, fishing excursions for Mr. Chambers, and shopping outings for Mrs. Chambers. Now its spotless surface, gleaming without so much as a speck of paper, let alone a letter from Lucian in response to the three letters a week she'd been sending him, left a lump of lead deep in Marigold's belly. A house that once rang with laughter was now far too quiet.

"Yes," she whispered, "I can leave."

But to what? She'd told Gordon Chambers she had somewhere to go. She did. At least she had a home with loving parents and a sister she got along with like a cherished friend. That sister, however, was getting married in two—

"Yoicks." Marigold's hands flew to her hair, pressing it flat.

She needed to tell Gordon Chambers immediately that she would have to be gone for a few days. Well. Perhaps she should stay home then, mend her fences with Lucian, force Gordon Chambers to stay with his nieces.

Mending matters with her fiancé should be a priority. She supposed he had reason to be distraught, when she'd made the girls her priority and postponed her wedding from the end of June until the beginning of October. She was

46

distraught. She wouldn't be the first McCorkle daughter to marry. She wouldn't get to keep the family heirloom that was still hers, since she was the first sister to become engaged—if she could still consider herself engaged. Thanks to her father's machinations in sending her off to be a servant for a year—to remind her of her family roots, to remind her she was not the gilded social princess she'd been acting like, much to her shame—and now her loyalty to Ruby and Beryl, she had probably lost that privilege unless something changed between her and Lucian soon—like receiving a letter from him saying he regretted his harsh words back in June—Marigold's plain, shy sister Rose would bear the honor of displaying the goldfinch bottle in her home.

Thanks to Gordon Chambers, too.

Hearing him in the library, Marigold continued through the foyer and down the short hall leading to the book-lined room. The door stood half open, framing him in an oblong of dark wood, with a backdrop of light from the windows. His back was to her—a long, straight back topped by broad, sturdy shoulders. At that moment, those shoulders were bent just a little, as though they bore a burden too heavy even for them, and his head was bowed, either in prayer or over some object he held.

As quietly as she could, Marigold slipped away. She could wait to tell him she was leaving for home in two weeks. If ever a man appeared as though he needed a few minutes alone, Gordon Chambers did in that glimpse through the half-open door.

For the first time since Gordon Chambers walked into his brother's house, Marigold considered his feelings in all of this. He'd lost his only brother, his twin. He had the responsibility of two little girls, though he was a bachelor who had lived on ships or in mining camps for nearly twelve years, and his personal plans had been interrupted. Even if he didn't intend to stow the girls in a boarding school like horses kept along a family's travel routes then ride off for the far-flung wilds of Alaska, his burdens must be numerous. He had to take care of the business for one thing. Surely he knew nothing of ledgers and balance sheets, supplies and boat repairs.

Well, maybe he knew about boats. But the rest? Marigold expected she knew more of accounting than Gordon Chambers did. She'd helped her father in their business during her summers away from school. She could add numbers faster in her head than someone with one of those new adding machines.

And as for his knowledge of children? Of course he had little. Yet he possessed something better than experience in taking care of little ones.

Kindness.

The way he'd treated his nieces since his arrival demonstrated that, for all his neglect of the past three months, the man's heart held tenderness for the little girls he'd never seen before.

"So how could he abandon them so abruptly?" Marigold slapped her fist into the palm of her other hand and headed up the steps.

At that moment, she was abandoning the girls for too long. She'd come downstairs to fetch Beryl's book left in the front parlor and gotten distracted by the lack of mail. That wouldn't do. The girls needed to keep up with their lessons, even if they weren't in school. Beryl sailed through her arithmetic, but Ruby needed a great deal of assistance with learning addition and subtraction, especially subtraction.

Gathering up the skirt of the gray gown she detested every morning she donned it to play nursemaid, as it made her skin too pale, Marigold raced up the steps to the schoolroom. Her feet pounded a little too loudly on the treads, and both girls greeted her in the corridor with censorious expressions.

"You aren't supposed to run in the house, Miss Marigold," Ruby chided.

"Do you have to write an essay about not running in the

house?" Beryl asked. "You made me do that the last time I ran up the steps."

"You're right, I did." Marigold rested a hand on each girl's shoulder and turned them to their work. "And I will do so, too."

"Why were you gone for so long?" Ruby plopped down in her miniature chair before the low table. "I thought maybe you got lost."

"She wouldn't get lost in the house." Beryl remained standing, her hands on her nonexistent hips. "Where's my book?"

Marigold caught her breath. "Your book. I forgot it."

Beryl sighed.

"I'll get it for you when we go downstairs for lunch." Marigold gestured to the other small chair at the table. "Sit down. We need to finish the math."

"I finished mine." Ruby held up her slate. "Beryl says I got two of them wrong, but I don't think so."

"Of course you don't think so." Beryl settled onto her chair and took Ruby's slate. "You wouldn't put down wrong answers if you thought they were wrong."

Marigold couldn't argue with that logic. But she couldn't let Beryl ridicule her younger sister, whose lower lip was trembling.

"Beryl, I will be the judge of Ruby's work. You need to be a little older to teach school."

"And get your answers all right all the time," Ruby added.

"No one is perfect." Marigold perched on the edge of an adult-sized chair and suppressed a sigh.

Perhaps she didn't know any more about children than did Gordon Chambers.

"Except for Jesus," she pointed out. "He was perfect."

"Can we read another Bible story after arithmetic?" Ruby asked.

"Yes." Marigold balanced Ruby's slate on her knees and examined the sums.

She did indeed have two problems wrong. The same kind of problems.

She was transposing numbers, writing eighteen instead of eighty-one and seventy-two instead of twenty-seven. The problem of nine. Too difficult for her, or a common difficulty with numbers that flipped around too easily?

Her grip tightened on the slate, and her jaw ached. She wasn't a teacher. She never intended to be a teacher. She wanted to be a wife, a mother, an artist good enough to draw designs for her husband's glasswork.

Instead, she was sitting in a stifling schoolroom smelling of chalk dust and cleaning polish. She was teaching two little girls who weren't her own, however much she cared about them. She'd stayed because their uncle couldn't be bothered to come home in a timely manner, demonstrating he didn't care about them, no matter how kind he'd been that morning.

"Miss Marigold?" Ruby's squeaky voice cut through Marigold's anger. "Are you going to cry?"

"Not now." Marigold made herself smile as she erased the two wrong numbers. "Let's start over with these two numbers. Beryl, you may go get your book and read until we're finished."

"May I sit on the window seat?" Beryl asked.

"Yes, you may." Marigold slipped to her knees so she was eye level with Ruby. "I think if you write down every number, you can keep them straight. . . ."

She and Ruby worked through the math problems until the child got all her answers right. Then the three of them went onto the back porch, where a cool breeze off the ocean rustled through the leaves of the sycamores shading the backyard. Marigold read from the book of Acts of the Apostles, where Paul is shipwrecked. She loved these times of reading scripture to the children. Ruby listened without sucking on her fingers, and Beryl made no derisive comments.

After a few minutes, Mrs. Cromwell joined them. When Marigold finished reading, they enjoyed lunch in the kitchen then returned to the schoolroom for reading lessons. Both girls liked books and read well according to their ages, and the time passed quickly.

Free to help Mrs. Cromwell with housework while the children played, Marigold allowed herself a sigh of relief, took the back steps two at a time, and missed the last step.

◆

Gordon caught the nursemaid's shoulders an instant before she slammed into him. Her nose connected with his chest, despite his efforts, and she reared back, one hand cupping the appendage.

"So solly," she mumbled from behind her hand. "I never expected—I shouldn't have been going so fast."

"Are you all right?" He tugged at her wrist to remove her hand and inspect the damage.

A slightly red, tip-tilted nose emerged. For a heartbeat, he experienced an odd urge to kiss it and make it better. But she was his nieces' governess, not one of them. A man didn't kiss the nose of a serving maid, even if she neither acted like nor, come to that, looked like anyone who had previously worked in the Chambers household.

Except for one, dear, sweet Louisa—

He jerked his hand away. "No blood, no damage."

"No, sir." She tucked her hair behind her ears, dislodging a pin. "Oh, dear." She stooped to retrieve it.

He stooped to retrieve it.

Their heads collided.

"I'm so sorry." She dropped onto the top step and buried her face in her hands. Her ridiculous hair tumbled and bobbed around her face. Her shoulders shook.

Gordon rocked back on his heels. "You aren't. . ." He cleared his throat. "This is nothing to cry about, Miss McCorkle."

"Not crying." She lifted her head. Although tears starred her lashes, her eyes danced with merriment. "I didn't know butting heads was literal."

"Nor I." Gordon's lips twitched into a full smile. His cheeks felt stiff and unnatural, bunched up and creased from the grin. Yet how did a body look at the absurd excuse for a governess or nursemaid and not come close to laughing aloud? "But what are we about to butt heads on, miss?"

Marigold sobered. "I was intending to speak to you about the girls sometime today, but this is when I usually help Mrs. Cromwell clean the house."

"Clean? What needs to be cleaned?" Gordon stood and offered Marigold his hand to help her rise.

She possessed rather elegant hands, slim and narrow with long, straight fingers. They were hands that should gleam white and feel as smooth as silk, but they held a hint of redness in their rough texture. Perhaps the abrasiveness against his own work-hardened hands explained the odd tingle he experienced as she rested her fingers in his palm and surged to her feet. A tingle and warmth. His mind conjured a fuse smoldering before it burst into flame and ignited the gunpowder that would blast another pile of rock apart to expose the precious metal inside.

He jerked away from her. "I have an appointment with the banker and my brother's attorney in a few minutes." He spoke with too much sharpness to dispel the ludicrous image from his brain. "We'll have to talk about the girls tomorrow. I'll know more of their financial situation at that time."

"But I want you to start overseeing their dinner instead of me." Marigold looked directly into his eyes. "They need to be with family now that they have one."

"I am hardly family." The image had exploded inside him, leaving the familiar hole that talk of family opened in his heart.

"You're their uncle."

"My brother was complicit in our father turning me out. That isn't family to me."

"Your brother made you their guardian in his will."

"He had little choice."

"He could have—" She snapped her lips shut like a clam-shell closing around its inhabitant.

Gordon narrowed his eyes. "Who else?"

"No one is better than family. Now, if you'll excuse me, there's laundry to do." She started to push past him.

He stepped in front of the door to the kitchen. "You didn't answer my question, Miss McCorkle."

"No, sir." She lowered her gaze to somewhere below his chin, as he was used to servants doing. "What Mr. Gerald Chambers decided to do with his daughters upon his and his wife's death is none of my concern. But I do need to tell you that I must be gone for several days in two weeks' time." Her words tumbled out in a rush as though she expected him to interrupt her. "My sister is getting married, and I am in the wedding, so you cannot leave then. I will send the girls down to dinner at six o'clock." Speech delivered, she stepped around him and slipped into the kitchen full of the aroma of roasting chicken.

"I'm not sure I'll be back—" The door swung shut on his protest.

He knew he should open the door again and dismiss her on the spot. If she wanted to be at her sister's wedding, he would give her plenty of time to get there.

But of course he wouldn't do that. No, he couldn't do that. He needed her here and she knew it. She knew it enough to take advantage of the truth and say whatever she liked, daring him to send her packing, as she deserved.

He supposed he could find another female to look after the girls, perhaps not keep them up with their schoolwork, if they even needed to in August, but make certain they were looked after and dressed neatly and washed behind their ears, all those minute details of children's lives, whatever they were. But he needed someone to care for them in a different way, the way Miss Marigold McCorkle cared for them—with love. He certainly wasn't capable of doing so to these offspring of his brother, who now possessed the inheritance that should have been at least half his.

All right, he would give Marigold her way. He would oversee the girls' dinner. He would stay until after she returned from her sister's wedding. He would stay until after the business sold.

If the business sold.

Thoughts of Dennis Tripp and his accusations replaced thoughts of Marigold McCorkle, keeping Gordon's mind occupied all the way to the bank.

The attorney met him there. With a clerk writing notes and dispensing various documents, Gordon spent two hours in the overcrowded office, with too much furniture and a ceiling fan that moved the air too slowly to do more than waft the odor of the macassar oil slicking back the banker's thinning hair into Gordon's face. He found himself growing drowsy as the attorney droned on, then the banker took his turn, then the attorney again. In the end, he learned exactly what he expected to learn—his brother had done well. Despite the financial panic of a half-dozen years earlier, his brother had grown their father's investments. The excursion boat company prospered in the months it was open, even managing to take a few tours out in finer weather throughout the year. Gerald had expanded the boats to making emergency runs across Delaware Bay to Philadelphia, for another profit source.

"Have you heard anything about a man named Dennis Tripp?" Gordon asked.

Both men shook their heads.

"He seems to be a disgruntled employee—former employee," Gordon explained. "He accosted me on the boardwalk this morning and told me that the manager is cheating the business by making false accounting entries about repairs."

"I wouldn't believe Tripp," the attorney said. "Lawrence Randall has been a faithful employee for nearly eight years."

"But feel free to look into the matter yourself, if you like," the banker added. "I can arrange to hire some accountants."

"No, thank you, I'll do it myself." Gordon noted the time. "I need to leave soon, but first, is it all right if I sell the boating business? And invest the money for the girls, of course."

The banker and attorney exchanged glances.

The latter cleared his throat. "I must not have made myself clear, Mr. Chambers. You can do whatever you like with the boating business. Your brother left it to you."

six

Marigold set her only good hat atop hair she had pomaded into submission and began to tilt the brim first one way then the other.

"Miss Marigold," Beryl called from the doorway, "we're going to be late for church if you don't hurry."

"Why are you taking so long?" Ruby asked from around her fingers.

"She wants to look nice for Uncle Gordon." Beryl giggled.

Marigold jammed the hat pin so hard it went through her pile of hair and pricked her scalp. She flinched. It served her right. Of course she was primping for Gordon Chambers, which was the most ridiculous action in the world. She was simply tired of him looking at her as though he didn't see her.

And no wonder. In her plain gray dresses, she looked dowdy and unattractive. She looked like what she was supposed to be—a servant. Only in her Sunday dress, one of the two gowns fit for church Father had allowed her to bring with her to Cape May—as part of her lesson in humility—did she deserve any notice. This Sunday she'd chosen the vivid green muslin that spread over her petticoats in rows of ruffles edged with fine, ivory embroidery. Matching green ribbons trailed from her hat brim and down her back.

"I can't go to church in my cleaning dresses," Marigold told the girls in defense of her finery. "I never have before."

"But you never changed your hat ribbons before." Beryl tilted her head to one side. "You look like a Christmas tree."

Ruby giggled.

So did Marigold. "Thank you for keeping me humble, child."

"What's humble?" Ruby asked.

56

"Hmm. Not proud." Marigold tried to think of a better explanation.

Something she wasn't, her father would say. Fifteen months in servitude hadn't changed that, as he'd intended.

"It means not putting yourself above others," Marigold concluded.

"If humble means wearing ugly dresses," Ruby said, "then I don't want to be humble."

"Humble is in your heart," Beryl said. "You can be prideful in an ugly dress. Like Miss Marigold."

"Maybe I will get taken down a peg or ten," Marigold grumbled then laughed. "All right, girls, I'm ready for church."

But not for the sight of Gordon Chambers in a fine new suit in a cream color that set off his tanned skin and dark hair. His image literally drove the air from her lungs. She gripped the newel post and tried to look past one of his broad shoulders, with a firm reminder that she was supposed to marry another man—someday.

Not that he'd written in response to her many letters.

"What a blessed man I am to have all these charming females to accompany me." Gordon smiled at his nieces and then Marigold.

Stomach suddenly queasy, Marigold made herself release the banister and glide forward. "We are all ready. Is Mrs. Cromwell coming today?"

"I'm right here, Marigold." The older woman stood beside Gordon.

Yoicks, she'd been there all along.

"Well, then, let's be on our way." Marigold offered a vapid smile all around.

She took hold of Ruby's and Beryl's hands and preceded Gordon and Mrs. Cromwell out the front door. The church stood only a few blocks away, so walking in the morning coolness proved easy and convenient. Others also walked: older husbands and wives arm in arm, mothers and fathers with flocks of small children, a few young people strolling in pairs. They greeted Marigold and the girls and cast curious or surprised glances at Gordon, who followed the younger women with Mrs. Cromwell on his arm.

He was such a gentleman. Despite a dozen years living in less than genteel locations, he must have learned a great deal as a young man, for Marigold could not fault his manners. He treated his nieces like princesses and Mrs. Cromwell like the loyal family retainer she was—with dignity and respect. For whatever reason he had left home and been reluctant to return, it surely wasn't because he lacked goodness in his heart.

Yet something tragic must have driven him away, kept him away, made him reluctant to return or stay. Occasionally, over the past week, she'd caught glimpses of pain on his face as he glanced at a photograph of his brother or parents, a tightening of his mouth at quiet intervals of the day.

Marigold he avoided, ignored, or simply pretended did not exist. She wasn't a lady, to him. She wasn't a relative. She wasn't a loyal family retainer. She wasn't a pretty girl. She wasn't even a girl anymore at twenty-five.

Papa, you might get your wish after all about me learning humility.

Especially if silence continued from Lucian and Gordon Chambers persisted in ignoring her. But no, Lucian would come around once she told him she was coming home for good soon, and Gordon should ignore her. She worked for him.

She shouldn't think about him. This was a time for worship, for thanking God for all He had done for her, like bringing Gordon to them at last, and for learning how to live her life better.

She held the girls' gloved hands more tightly and led them up the steps of the church. The pastor greeted them. Many other little girls spoke to Beryl and Ruby. They were with their parents, who nodded at Marigold, started to speak, then stopped, eyes widening.

"It's my uncle Gordon," Ruby announced to the foyer at

large. "He's come back after a long time, so I think Mommy and Daddy will, too."

The foyer fell silent. A handful of women drew handkerchiefs from their pocketbooks and dabbed at their eyes. Men cleared their throats and kept their gazes on a point behind Marigold—Gordon, she presumed.

He stepped forward and took Ruby's hand in his. "Your mommy and daddy won't be coming back here to Cape May like I did, sweetheart, but if you keep trusting in Jesus, you can go to them when it's your time to do so."

A collective sigh nearly slammed the door. Marigold's own heart felt squeezed. She didn't blame the females in the room who gazed at Gordon Chambers as though he were the most important man alive. At that moment, in that church entryway, he was.

"But I want to see them now," Ruby protested amid a rising wave of murmuring voices.

"Be quiet." Beryl cast her little sister a scornful glance. "You sound like a spoiled baby."

"And you sound unkind," Marigold whispered to Beryl. "Let your uncle take care of Ruby."

"But she gets all his attention acting so silly." Beryl stuck out her lower lip.

"She doesn't do it on purpose."

At least Marigold didn't think Ruby was playacting to get her uncle's attention.

"She's still sad about your mother and father."

"I am, too." Tears started in Beryl's eyes. "But I know what dead means and so does she."

"I'm not sure she does." Marigold squeezed Beryl's hand and tugged her forward, into the throng now surrounding Gordon and Ruby.

Mrs. Cromwell had slipped away to join her sister and some other older ladies.

"I'm a lot older than she is, and I don't know how sad she is," Marigold added.

She had grown fond of her employers over the year she lived with them, but they were employers, not friends, not people with whom she socialized, except on those rare occasions when someone who knew her family happened to be in Cape May and invited her, too. It was awkward, but Mr. and Mrs. Chambers were so gracious that they'd never asked her not to accept invitations, though Gerald Chambers had done business with Marigold's father and agreed to hire his wayward, prideful daughter for a year.

Though the Chamberses knew Marigold was supposed to remember she came from folks who knew life serving the wealthy, not being served, they encouraged her to go to parties. Marigold wearing the same dresses to every occasion was her humiliation. Katherine Chambers, who had been married at eighteen and a mother by nineteen, had worried about Marigold being in her twenties and barely engaged, had tried to give her gowns. Marigold had refused and accepted the scornful glances of ladies recognizing a dress thrice worn. Marigold did have a fiancé. Lucian proposed to her in March of 1898 and received her father's permission. Albeit his reluctant, hesitant permission. Marigold had gotten her pride from somewhere, and Father wanted more for her than a glassblower's apprentice, however talented.

She wondered if Father hoped the marriage plans would end with the year-long separation. He never said so, but perhaps he had asked the Chamberses to find her another beau, see that she married someone more suitable in his eyes. If they held that responsibility, they should have lived so Marigold could be married now, perhaps on her way to being a mother.

The flash of annoyance took Marigold's breath away. She hadn't realized she could be angry with two people who weren't alive. She hadn't realized she was angry at all. She loved Ruby and Beryl. She wanted to see them happy and settled before she started her new life with Lucian.

At the moment, she wanted to see them settled for the

service. The swirl of people around Gordon and Ruby seemed likely to make that impossible. With a sinking sensation in her middle, she glanced from Gordon, his head visible above a garden of ladies' hats, to Beryl then back again.

"Go join your uncle, Beryl," Marigold said on a sigh. "I'll sit somewhere else today. Be sure to say excuse me if you have to go between two people."

Beryl gave her a pointed look and slipped away.

Marigold followed the crowd into the sanctuary, as she must today and every Sunday Gordon Chambers remained in Cape May. Marigold couldn't sit with him and the children. It wouldn't look right. When Mr. and Mrs. Chambers had been alive, Marigold had joined the family. That was expected. She was there to see to the children's needs. But a single female and single man could not share a pew without arousing gossip, harmful gossip with Marigold living in the house, however good a job Mrs. Cromwell performed as a chaperone.

Longing to be home with her family and friends, Marigold slipped into a pew near the back. She must remember that this was a time of worship, not socializing. She didn't need to have loved ones around her to pray and sing hymns and listen to the sermon. In an hour and a half, she would rejoin the girls for the walk home, for their Sunday dinner, for quiet activity reading or playing the piano.

Presently she felt lost in a church she'd attended for over a year. No one was unfriendly. They simply weren't cordial beyond an initial nod and acknowledgment of her presence. She was a nursemaid, a temporary fixture, as was more than half the congregation. Most of them remained in Cape May for no more than the hot summer months.

She'd worn her second prettiest dress and gone to the trouble of changing the ribbons on her hat for nothing. God didn't care what she looked like.

Hot in the layers of ruffles, Marigold nearly fell asleep during the sermon. Although she managed to stay awake, she couldn't keep her mind on the thread of the pastor's subject. She heard her father instead, reminding her of vanity, of pride, her overabundance of both.

When the service ended, she made herself remain seated, her hands clasped in her lap, until nearly everyone else had filed out. Gordon and the girls passed by early in the recessional. Ruby waved, but Beryl pulled her along; two attractive young women in pastel gowns and blond curls followed so closely behind that Marigold couldn't have stepped out of her pew if she'd been standing.

Gordon Chambers, the Pied Piper of Cape May.

Smiling, Marigold slipped into the aisle and exited the church.

"Miss McCorkle?"

Marigold turned at the sound of her name. "Mr. Tripp?"

She knew the man as a regular attendee of the church, but he'd never approached her before.

He gave her a courtly bow then stepped closer than strictly necessary for polite conversation. "I apologize for waylaying you, but I am concerned about the Chambers Excursion and Sailing Company. I approached Mr. Chambers, but he hasn't heeded my warning."

"Warning?" Marigold looked into the man's gentle gray eyes and frowned. "What are you talking about?"

"I warned him about Mr. Randall claiming he's repairing the boats but not doing it. When I approached him about it, he dismissed me."

"I see."

"No, I don't think you do. I'm not a disgruntled employee seeking revenge. I care about people's lives."

He looked sincere—and worried.

"I don't have any influence over Mr. Chambers. I'm nothing more than an employee myself."

And not a highly regarded one.

"But I'll try to see if he's doing anything, Mr. Tripp."

"Thank you." His smile lit his haggard face.

Insides uneasy, Marigold scanned the crowd for the family. Because of his height, she spotted Gordon straightaway. He stood on the front walk talking with a middle-aged couple Marigold recognized with an uplifting of her heart and a hastening of her steps.

"Mr. and Mrs. Morris!" The cry left her lips before she could stop herself.

They, Gordon, and too many congregants turned to stare at her.

Her cheeks heated. "I beg your pardon." She skidded to a halt a yard from the group. "I was just so happy to see you. . . ."

"No pardon necessary." Paul Morris took Marigold's hands in his and squeezed them between his strong fingers.

His wife kissed Marigold on the cheek. "You look lovely, child. We're staying only three houses from the Chambers' place, so you must come visit."

"I will, if I can." Marigold glanced at Gordon.

"I believe you're entitled to time off." He looked half amused and half bemused.

"Then come down whenever you can. We'll catch you up on all the news of home. But now we must rush off." Mrs. Morris, petite and with more silver in her hair than gilt, turned back to Gordon and the girls. "We'll expect you next Saturday night then, Mr. Chambers. And when my great-nieces and nephews come to visit next week," she added to the girls, "you all must come down to play. There are quite a lot of them, you know, so you ought to find one of them you like." She squeezed Marigold's hand. "I'll talk to you later, my dear."

Leaving the girls and Marigold smiling, the Morrises bade good day and headed down the sidewalk.

"They're nice," Ruby announced around her fingers.

"Their great-nieces are all Ruby's age. The only person my age is a boy." Beryl swept toward the sidewalk with the air of a grande dame wearing a ball gown.

Gordon met Marigold's eyes, and they shared a smile that made a butterfly take off in her belly.

"How long before she changes her mind about that?" he asked.

"Four or five years?"

Marigold wasn't about to admit she never went through a time when she didn't think boys were great companions. She'd been nearly as good at baseball as any of the Morris or Grassick boys.

"How do you know the Morrises?" Gordon asked Marigold as he steered Ruby after Beryl. "Do they come to Cape May every year?"

"Yes, but I grew up knowing them. That is. . ." Marigold took a risky plunge. "My great-grandmother worked for Paul Morris's parents."

It was strictly the truth, just not all of the truth.

"Interesting." The look Gordon Chambers gave her, his dark brows arched over those deep eyes, told Marigold he knew she wasn't telling him everything.

But he *was* looking at her.

"Is it all right if I call on them?" she asked.

"Of course. Whenever you like. Mrs. Cromwell can watch after the girls some, too."

"Or you could."

"I already do." His voice turned dry. "And speaking of Mrs. Cromwell, where is she?"

"She always goes to her sister's house on Sunday afternoons. Didn't she tell you?"

"No. Um, what do we do for dinner?"

"I cook." Marigold laughed at the shock on his face. "I was teasing about the bread and eggs. I'm rather good at it, I'll have you know."

"Not in that, I hope." Though the look he gave her barely touched on her hat, then face, then gown, a tingling warmth in her tummy warned her to watch her step.

She hovered close to the edge of being disloyal to Lucian.

As soon as they reached home, she changed back into one of her gray gowns. The girls pulled pinafores over their good dresses and went into the garden to sit beneath the trees, Beryl with a book and Ruby with her slate and colored chalks. Where Gordon slunk off to Marigold neither knew nor cared—or so she told herself. She needed to cook.

She knew how to make exactly two meals well, besides bread and eggs, which he would learn if he were around many more Sundays. Today it would be roast beef with carrots, potatoes, and onions. She also made passable biscuits. Fresh blueberries would serve for dessert.

By the time the girls and their uncle seated themselves at the dining table, Marigold was hot and perspiring, with her hair either in tight corkscrews or as fuzzy as mohair. But the vegetables were tender, the meat juicy, and the biscuits flaky.

"Enjoy yourselves." She set the dishes on the table in front of Gordon. "I'll start washing up."

"You aren't going to eat?" Gordon asked.

He apparently wouldn't dream of inviting her to join them, and she wouldn't invite herself and risk being rebuffed.

She smiled. "When I finish cooking, I have no interest in eating. I'll make a sandwich out of the leftover meat."

"What if we eat it all?" Ruby giggled.

"We can't eat that much." Beryl gave the roast a disdainful glance.

"We'll try not to." Gordon reached out his hands to the girls. "Shall we bless this meal?"

Dismissed without the words, Marigold retreated to the kitchen then continued to the relative coolness on the back porch. A few minutes in the shade and breeze wouldn't hurt anyone. She flopped onto the steps and fanned herself with the hem of her apron. She must talk to Gordon about Dennis Tripp's admonition concerning the boats. It was likely nothing. Gerald Chambers had trusted Lawrence Randall, his manager, implicitly, allowing him the primary operation of the business. In fact, the late Mr. Chambers had rarely gone to the company's office. He didn't seem to like it much.

So Mr. Tripp could be right. Gordon, of course, wouldn't

want anything to do with it, if he wanted to move on as fast as he could. . . .

Well, he just couldn't move on, whatever his reasons. She would stop him somehow. Leaving the girls without family was wrong and—

"Marigold?" Mrs. Morris called from the back gate. "Is that you?"

"It is." Marigold descended the steps and crossed the lawn to greet the older lady over the wicket. "What brings you down the alley?"

"I was taking the shortcut from visiting some friends down the way." The older lady's bright blue eyes scanned Marigold from head to foot, growing troubled as they did so. "My dear, why do you continue this masquerade? Your father only required a year of service for you."

"I couldn't abandon the children. They're so. . .lost without their parents, and their uncle—" Marigold's hands tightened on the top bar of the gate.

"But you put these children before your marriage. Are you sure that was the right choice?"

"Would leaving them to no familiar faces except for Mrs. Cromwell's been the right choice?"

"They have an uncle."

"Who couldn't be bothered to come home." The gate bar creaked.

Mrs. Morris laid her hand, soft in its silk glove, atop Marigold's. "If you'd told him what you had to sacrifice, perhaps he would have come sooner."

"I wasn't sacrificing really." Marigold gazed past Mrs. Morris to the glint of the sea. "This is a grand place to spend the summer, as you know. And I love the girls."

"But you made a promise to Lucian."

"Lucian," Marigold enunciated, her chin lifted, "needs to understand about patience and giving, if he wants to marry me."

"Yes. Yes, he must." Mrs. Morris frowned. "Perhaps that's why. . . Has he written to you?"

"Not in weeks."

And that letter had been impatient and demanding.

"Well, it doesn't matter now." Mrs. Morris's brow still lay in deep furrows. "I've come to tell you that he is sailing into town with my daughter and son-in-law tomorrow."

seven

By Monday morning, Gordon knew his idea of leaving within two weeks was ridiculous. He still didn't know if he gave any credence to Dennis Tripp's warning, but before putting the business up for sale, even if he trusted an agent to oversee the particulars, Gordon couldn't hire an agent without being certain the business was sound.

The problem he was encountering lay in finding the discrepancies in Lawrence Randall's bookkeeping. Twice he presented himself at the boating office. Both times, Randall was out, either on one of the excursion boats, according to the clerks, or at the bank. They didn't feel right giving him the ledgers without asking Mr. Randall which ones were the right ones.

"That is the one for this year," one of the mousy little men clarified. "Since Mr. Chambers has been gone. The other Mr. Chambers, that is."

The third time, that Monday morning, when Mr. Randall just happened to be absent, Gordon made his way to the attorney's office to ask what recourse he could take.

"You have a right to the books, of course." The rather youthful-looking Mr. Phillips, attorney-at-law, drew off his spectacles, making him look even younger. "Just take whichever ones you like. Randall has no right to stop you. But the real problem you're facing is that you can't sell the business until the will is probated."

"Probated? I thought—" Gordon subsided onto a chair he'd refused to take a few minutes earlier. "I thought that had already been done."

"No, it'll take a few more months to go through the court. Your long absence slowed matters. I thought you would know this." Phillips raised his eyebrows.

Gordon resisted the urge to squirm like a schoolboy caught not knowing his lessons. "I've never inherited anything before."

"Of course. Then let me explain."

Gordon listened and wondered if he would get to Alaska before the great glaciers melted. Or before he melted from the heat.

At last freed, he returned to the house to find a stack of invitations awaiting him in a silver bowl that resided on the foyer table. Apparently mindful that he was in mourning for his brother, none of the invitations were objectionable, being quiet and small affairs, but Gordon cringed at the idea of accepting any of them. They would first gasp at his resemblance to Gerald, as many had done in church. They would then ask about what he'd been doing for the past dozen years, why he had gone away, what he would be doing now, why he had stayed away for months after his brother's death—all questions too painful to think about, let alone discuss. Besides that, single young women would swarm around him, an affluent eligible bachelor in their eyes, and he would want to head for the nearest boat and out to sea.

He'd felt that way in church: stifled, hemmed in, trapped. He wanted to forget about his life in Cape May, not recall every childhood memory. He certainly didn't want to get into a young lady's clutches simply by being too polite to her.

He didn't want to encounter anyone who might know why he'd been asked to leave home and been cut out of his father's will. At the same time, he couldn't ignore the invitations. Good manners had been drilled into his head deeply enough he hadn't lost them in the roughest of living conditions. He'd enjoyed comfort from the knowledge he wasn't shaming his mother's teachings, even if his father thought him a failure as a good and obedient son.

He spread the invitations out on the table. He needed advice on which ones he absolutely could not reject and which ones he could get away with declining. Perhaps Marigold—

No, the less time spent with that minx the better. She was a bold piece, brazen in her manner toward him. She acted as though she didn't care in the least whether or not she pleased him.

No, on second thought, she wasn't acting. She didn't care if she pleased him or not.

A reluctant smile tugged at his lips. Odd for a nursemaid—but refreshing amid fawning females. Even the men seemed to want to see him happy. And now the hostesses had left their mark in the form of too many invitations for a man who preferred to spend his days alone.

Alone was safer.

With a flick of his wrist, he sent the invitations flying into a disorderly pile and turned from the table.

"You can't ignore them, you know—sir." Marigold came around the end of the staircase, a stack of clean rags over one arm, a pot of something reeking of lemon and beeswax clutched in her other hand. She wore another one of those hideous gray dresses, and an enormous white kerchief nearly covered her hair.

His fingers twitched, and he clasped his hands behind his back to stop himself from snatching the cloth from her hair. The action would not only be rude and obtrusive, it was an absurd idea. She should keep that mop covered all the time, if that's what it took to control the wild red mass.

"Mr. and Mrs. Morris invited you personally yesterday," Marigold continued, "so ignoring them would be unconscionable."

"Thank you for your advice." He didn't keep the edge of sarcasm from his tone. "I was brought up in a barn, you know."

"I know no such thing. But you have been away from civilization for a while."

"And would like to be away from it again, if it's all as vapid as this." He waved one hand at the invitations.

"The Morrises aren't vapid. They're smart and amusing and love the Lord." She began to polish the newel post, turning her profile to him. "And one of Mr. Morris's sisters is married to a Grassick."

"Is that supposed to impress me?"

"No, not if you don't know who they are. I'm sorry to interfere." Her voice sounded suddenly thick.

"Miss Marigold?" Gordon stepped closer to her before he realized his intention. "Is something the matter?"

She shook her head. A red curl popped out from under the kerchief.

He touched a fingertip to the tear tracing down her cheek. "Then the polish is too strong and making your eyes water."

"No, I—it doesn't concern you. Excuse me, please. This banister gets terribly dusty with the windows open." Wafting the nose-tickling scent of lemon behind her, she plowed up the steps, her head bowed, her face hidden.

Gordon watched her for several moments, seeking words to make her come back, while wondering why he should care. He couldn't befriend her. He didn't dare. Even if a friendship between master and employee was appropriate, which it wasn't, he was no good as a friend, as a brother, son, uncle. . . .

He returned to the table, gathered up the invitations, and carried them into the library. Of the twelve, he accepted three. The dinner party at the home of Mr. and Mrs. Paul Morris was the first one—on Saturday. The other two were invitations to nights of music. He loved music, and all he'd heard since returning to Cape May, other than the hymns in church, were his nieces' painful renditions on the piano and Marigold singing Christmas carols in August.

They were young. They would learn. He suspected Miss Marigold wasn't the best of music teachers. All the more reason to find them a school.

With that in mind, he accepted a fourth invitation, to a luncheon with just men, business associates of his brother and people he'd been introduced to at church. Reintroduced to. Some of them probably had daughters in school, judging from their ages. He could talk to them about where to send the girls.

He needed to talk with them about something. Long social conversations weren't among his talents. Talking to anyone for more than half an hour hadn't been part of his life for so long that dinners with his nieces left him feeling exhausted. After an initial shyness, they'd begun to ask him questions and wouldn't settle for the concise responses he gave adults.

❧

"No, Uncle Gordon, tell us how you got back on the ship after you fell in the water," Beryl insisted.

"Did you do something bad?" Ruby asked. "Is that why God made you fall?"

"God didn't make me fall, child." Gordon gazed at the little girl, wondering how she got such a notion. "I made myself fall by not putting away the rope I'd been splicing together. I tripped over it and... Splash!"

"But how did you get back aboard?" Beryl persisted.

"Someone saw me fall and sent me a line." Gordon grimaced at the memory. "It's a good thing the water was calm."

"Because you were naughty?" Ruby asked.

Beryl cast her a glance of annoyance. "People don't drown because they're naughty."

"But—"

"Mommy and Daddy weren't bad," Beryl continued with dogged ruthlessness.

Gordon flinched. Perhaps he hadn't chosen a good story. Next time—

He couldn't think about next time. Ruby had begun to cry.

"Not again," Beryl groaned, but her own eyes shimmered with tears.

Marigold! Gordon cried silently.

As though she heard him anyway, she swept through the door leading into the kitchen, dressed in a plain but attractive dress of white with little pink flowers on it, and dropped to her knees beside Ruby. "It's all right, baby. No one's been naughty."

"I was," Ruby wailed. "I left my doll outside in the rain."

Over Ruby's shoulder, Gordon met Marigold's eyes. She looked as bewildered as he felt.

They hadn't had rain in the week he'd been back in Cape May.

"Your doll is in your room." Beryl pushed her plate aside. "I would like dessert, please. Mrs. Cromwell said we have ice cream."

"We have to go get it. Would you like that, Ruby?" Marigold tugged one of the girl's pigtails.

Ruby blinked away her tears. "I like strawberry ice cream. But I only get it if I'm good."

"You're good." Marigold rose, holding Ruby's hand. "You even got your arithmetic right today. Are you going with us, Mr. Chambers?"

"I think I must."

He didn't want to. In the cool of early evening, the streets would be crowded with vacationers swarming toward ice cream shops and soda fountains for refreshing treats after dinner or on their way home from the beach. But he felt responsible for Ruby's bout of tears and thought the least he could do was take her for ice cream.

Alone.

"You don't need to come with us, Miss Marigold," he said.

Her face tightened, whether with annoyance, anger, or hurt he couldn't tell, for she smiled immediately. "I wasn't going to go with you, Mr. Chambers. I have. . . I have a guest calling tonight."

"Indeed?" Gordon raised his eyebrows in query.

Marigold turned to the children. "Go wash your hands, girls."

A note had arrived from Mrs. Morris in the middle of the afternoon, warning Marigold that Lucian had reached Cape May. A message from him had arrived shortly afterward with the information that he would call upon her that evening after supper. An appeal to Mrs. Cromwell's kindness had arranged the ice cream expedition.

"It's about time you saw that young man you've moped over for the past year," the older lady had declared.

So Marigold donned a dress suitable for everyday wear, a step above her gray maid's dress, and paced from the library to the music room to the front parlor, waiting, praying, willing Lucian to call before Gordon Chambers and the girls returned. And waiting. . . And waiting. . .

Mrs. Cromwell had cleared away the supper dishes and gone to her room by the time a rap sounded on the back door. Marigold flew down the hall, through the baize-covered door and through the spotless kitchen.

Spotless except for the puddle of water where the icebox pan had overflowed. Her right foot landed in the pool and slipped. She flung out her arms for balance, dislodged a copper pan hanging on the wall, and slammed her shoulder into the door. The pan flew across the room with a resounding clang, and her cry of pain accompanied the thud of her body striking wood.

"Marigold?" Lucian called through the portal. "Is that you?" He opened the door, and she tumbled into his arms.

"So sorry." She clung to him, his sturdy shoulders, his arms wiry with tensile strength. She smiled up into his handsome face and waited for the rush of warmth she'd always experienced when near him, the thrill of being in his presence.

The only heat she experienced was a flush of embarrassment for her clumsy introduction to a man she hadn't seen since his last visit in June, the day he'd arrived to persuade her to leave, to go ahead with their wedding regardless of the inconvenience to the girls.

The day he'd suggested she take off her engagement ring until she had her priorities straightened out.

She rubbed her bare finger and scanned him for the lump of a ring box in his pocket. Seeing nothing, feeling a little unwell, she said, "I expected you at the front door."

"I wasn't aware servants could receive callers in the front."

The merest hint of a sneer curled his upper lip.

"It would be all right here. Mr. Chambers isn't strict or all that formal."

"Humph." He laid his hands on her shoulders and set her from him. "What was all that racket?"

"Just me being a bit clumsy." Marigold shrugged. "Shall we go onto the porch? No one else is home except for Mrs. Cromwell, and she's in her room. Would you like some lemonade?"

"No, thank you, I won't be here long."

"No?" Marigold gripped the edge of the door to support her now wobbly knees. "Do you—do you have another engagement?"

"I may." He turned and strode to one of the wrought iron chairs scattered around the wide veranda. "It all depends on your answers."

"Well, since I haven't heard the questions, I guess I can't give you those answers, can I?" Marigold didn't intend the note of asperity that slipped out.

At the moment, with Lucian showing no affection toward her, she felt no inclination to take back the words or apologize for the tone.

Lucian laughed as though she'd made a joke. "Let's be comfortable so I can ask them." He turned one of the chairs so she faced the sliver of ocean visible between the neighboring houses.

She settled herself and waited for him to sit.

He didn't. He leaned against the white-painted railing and faced her. Evening light gleamed in his blond hair. His countenance lay in shadow. "When are you coming home?" he demanded.

"When things are settled here." Marigold clasped her hands hard enough to hurt her fingers. "I think Mr. Chambers will hire someone else, but it takes time. Perhaps October?" She hated the uncertainty in her voice, the queasiness in her stomach. "I know it's a long time, but—"

"It's too long. We were supposed to be married at the end of June. Do you know how embarrassing it is for me to have to tell people my fiancée thinks more of some children than me?"

"Perhaps as embarrassing as it is for me to keep telling my friends I never hear from you."

"I have work in Salem County to keep me busy."

"And so do I."

"You don't need to. Your father said a year away to make sure I—" He snapped his teeth together and paced to the end of the porch and back, his hands clasped behind his back.

Marigold stared at him, her ears buzzing. "To make sure you what?"

"Never mind." He bit out the words like someone eating a distasteful dish. "You were sent here to these business associates of your father because you needed to be reminded of your humble roots before marrying a mere glassblower." Now the bitterness rang as loud and clear as the crickets in the grass chirped with the advent of sunset.

Head spinning, Marigold rose and approached him. "Lucian, it's not like that at all. I got above myself, was mean to my sister, was too proud of marrying—"

"So you could get the goldfinch first." Now the sneer was more than a hint. "I'd say your father is the one who needs to remember his humble roots, far more humble than the original Grassicks."

"No one looks down at even apprentice glassblowers now, Lucian. You're artists, as well as artisans. Half the Grassick family are glassblowers. You can't think my father. . . ."

Apparently that was exactly what he thought.

Marigold held out her hands to him. "My dear, yes, my father sent me here to learn humility—"

"To get you away from me—"

"And I just can't leave these children—"

"Who are more important than I am."

"No, no, Mr. Chambers wants me to leave." Marigold swallowed against a rising lump in her throat, took a deep breath against the band that seemed to tighten around her chest. "I'll be home for Rose's wedding. I—I'll stay home then."

"Do what you like." Lucian strode to the porch steps. With his back to her, he added, "I just came calling tonight to tell you I'm seeing someone else."

୬

With two clean hands in his, Gordon walked to the nearest ice cream parlor amid a throng of other families bent on the same enjoyment. Though many people smiled at him and nodded, he knew none of them, and they seemed not to know Gerald. None of them spoke to him.

Strawberry ice cream for Ruby and vanilla for Beryl obtained and consumed, Gordon took two sticky hands in his and returned home. Ruby chattered the whole way, as though she'd never shed a tear in her life.

Beryl said little beyond thanking him for the dessert. He wondered if he'd said something to upset her now. But when they reached the house, she ran halfway up the steps, then turned around and blew him a kiss. "You're a good uncle," she announced, "even if you took too long to get here and want to leave us again."

"You can't leave," Ruby wailed.

At that moment, with her big blue eyes gazing into his, he thought she was right.

"We won't worry about that now, Ruby." He patted her head. "Go on up and get your hands washed before you stain your dress."

"All right." She, too, blew him a kiss and raced up the steps like an awkward colt.

Out of sight, the girls grew out of mind, or at least sentimental feeling. His brother might have made Gordon their guardian because he was their only living relative, but Gerald wouldn't want Gordon to raise them. Gerald had known his brother seemed to only hurt those he cared about, whatever his good intentions.

Gordon supposed Marigold McCorkle could stay on and see to the majority of their upbringing. That wasn't unusual. Perhaps it was even better than sending them to a school. But that meant he would have to stay, and Alaska called. Gold called. The wild aloneness called. A man could think in air that fresh and clean and devoid of people. He didn't want to worry about anyone else's troubles. His own had consumed him long enough. Right now, working out if anything was wrong with the business consumed him.

Wednesday morning he went down to the boathouse and inspected the crafts bobbing at their moorings along the pier. All appeared clean and shiny. Paint gleamed white; the names in gold leaf caught the sun and the eye. Brass shimmered. But fresh paint was easily applied and could merely be an illusion of good repair.

Yet why should he believe this Dennis Tripp, a man dismissed from his job, over a longtime and reliable employee like Lawrence Randall? The answer was simple—he shouldn't. Tripp merely wanted revenge against the man who'd sent him packing. Still. . .

Gordon knocked on the office door then pushed it open.

"Mr. Chambers." The clerks greeted him cheerfully. "We have your ledgers ready for you."

"Well, uh, thank you." Gordon felt a flush of embarrassment for his doubt of the manager creeping up his neck. "That's thoughtful of you."

"It's not a problem, sir. Do you want someone to carry them back to the house for you?"

"No, thank you, I can manage." He lifted the stack of account books from the clerk's arms. "I'll bring them back as soon as possible."

"No hurry." The clerk smiled.

So did his companions.

Gordon frowned on his way out the door. Though fifty pounds of ledgers filled his arms, uneasiness nagged at his middle. Yes, Randall had voluntarily given up the books, yet not wanting them back immediately struck a discordant note in Gordon's mind. This made no sense. An accountant should want the books back immediately. He should need them to refer back to and add on to, as the business was still open and current—

Ah, that was it. Gordon hadn't received the current books.

Jaw set, he marched the rest of the way home and slammed the books onto the desk. A gasp caught his attention. Marigold, her hair restrained by a lacy cap—that would have looked better on Mrs. Cromwell—and wearing a gown that made her skin look the color of a fish's belly, knelt in front of one of the bookcases, a heavy tome in her hands.

"Did I startle you?" he asked.

"Yes." She rose. "I didn't expect you to slam those books down."

"I didn't slam—" He stopped and scowled.

He didn't need to explain or apologize for his actions. It was his house, until the girls turned twenty-one. This was his office and his desk. Females wanted to interfere, introduce themselves into a man's life even when he didn't need one, and make him feel like he'd done something wrong because he made a little noise.

He glanced at her book. "Isn't Elizabeth Gaskell's work a little old for my nieces?"

"It's not for your nieces. It's for me." That said, she turned on her heel and stalked from the room.

Gordon stared at her. He'd never met such an uppity female, not even in the West, where women tended to have freer spirits than in the East. She had no right—

Well, he'd just dismiss her. Finding someone else to look after the girls was going to be difficult and cause yet more delays, but Marigold McCorkle had to go. He wanted a female who moved around unobtrusively like Mrs. Cromwell, one whose company he could seek out, if he wanted it.

Which he wouldn't. He never sought out anyone's company. He had in the past and caused too much trouble.

Shoving the ledgers to one end of the desk, Gordon rounded the massive structure and dropped into a chair. He found paper and a fountain pen in one of the drawers. After filling the pen, he composed an advertisement for the local paper. He also found the name of an employment bureau among some of the household books stashed in the desk. That might be easier than advertising. They would be able to send qualified candidates without him having to interview a dozen females to discover if they were suitable to care for his nieces. Perhaps he should ask the pastor.

Messages to the agency and pastor composed, Gordon pulled the top book from the stack of ledgers and began to work. He worked until his eyes burned and his stomach growled. Somewhere in the house, a clock chimed just once. He didn't know if that meant a half hour or one o'clock. As if in response, the library door swung open and the smell of mushroom soup preceded Marigold into the room.

"I brought you your lunch." She set the tray on a table before the empty fireplace. "Would you like coffee afterward?"

"I would, thank you." Gordon rose.

Marigold started for the door.

"Miss Marigold?"

She stopped, didn't turn, but tilted her head in a listening attitude.

"Why are you wearing that cap all of a sudden?" he demanded.

Her hands flew to the unbecoming headgear. "Mrs. Chambers had all of us wear caps to keep our hair out of the food and from falling over the house. I stopped after she. . . It's hot and I hate it, but it's disrespectful not to wear it."

"And when"—he closed the distance between them—"did you start worrying about being disrespectful?"

She raised her gaze to his, and he flinched at the sadness that clouded their bright color. "Since I realized that perhaps I'm better off staying here with the girls than going. . .home. Now, if you'll excuse me, I'll fetch that coffee."

Before he thought up an appropriate response, she whisked

from the room, the full skirt of her dress lingering behind her like the tail of a gray mouse.

Not that anything about Marigold was mousy. She could wear all the gray dresses and caps she liked. A girl with her demeanor could never come across as timid.

Gordon found himself smiling as he carried his lunch to the desk and continued running his own calculations through the books. A few more hours of the work, and he wasn't smiling at all. The walls closed in on him. The air stifled him. He yawned and longed for a long ride in the open, or perhaps a sail across the bay and back.

He would take one, a moonlight sail. Someone should have a boat he could rent.

Hearing the girls playing the piano, he made his way to the music room and tapped on the door.

"Uncle Gordon." Ruby slid off the bench and raced to hug him. "I haven't seen you all day."

"I've been busy."

And he shouldn't feel a pang of guilt.

"And now I'm going to leave for a few hours," he told her.

"You're not dressed for a dinner party," Beryl pronounced.

"I'm going sailing." He addressed this to Marigold, who stood behind the piano.

"Sailing?" Ruby clutched his hand. "You can't go sailing, Uncle Gordon. I was naughty today."

eight

Marigold stood at the front parlor window and pounded her fists against her legs. She should have been down on her knees praying for her soul, for forgiveness, for the ability to like Mr. Gordon Chambers. But at that moment, watching him stride toward the house at nearly two o'clock in the morning, she wanted to yank open the front door and shove him down the steps.

"If you want to be alone," she mouthed to the fluid shadow of the man, "then leave. Give us access to money this time, and we'll do just fine without you."

If Mrs. Cromwell weren't so determined to leave New Jersey for a warmer climate, Marigold would have said that. Now she had no reason to go home. Lucian had betrayed her. He hadn't waited as he promised. Going home meant facing people's pity, the kind of sympathy she'd witnessed in Mrs. Morris's eyes.

Except Marigold had to go home for her sister's wedding. The pity would be rampant there. She was the daughter who'd gotten engaged first. She should have wed before Rose. She should have the family heirloom now residing in her dresser at home. But because of the man now climbing the front steps, Marigold was a spinster too angry to sleep or pray or even speak to the man.

"But you could have stayed home for Ruby's sake." She ground her teeth and drew into the shadows of the parlor so he didn't catch a glimpse of her and feel inclined to speak. At the moment, she intended to practice the premise that if she could say nothing nice, she should keep her mouth shut. Let Ruby make him feel his guilt.

Not that the child had been able to when he announced he

was leaving. She'd started crying too hard to have any of her words coherent. When Gordon tried to comfort her, she'd turned her face away from him and reached for Marigold. She caught a glimpse of hurt in his eyes—or thought she did. The fact that he'd simply said, "I'll be late," and departed made Marigold doubt her own judgment in what she'd witnessed of his expression.

After a few moments of Ruby crying, Beryl announced, "She's afraid of water."

"And Uncle Gordon's going on the water," Ruby said through hiccups.

"He'll be all right." Marigold made the promise, knowing too late what would follow.

"Mommy and Daddy weren't." Ruby stopped crying but grew quiet and ate little dinner.

Afterward, Marigold took her into the garden to play with Dahlia, the kitten, and a ball of yarn. When both child and kitten flopped onto the grass exhausted, Marigold settled beside them and asked why Ruby told Uncle Gordon not to leave because she'd been naughty.

"You weren't even naughty," Marigold concluded. "All you did was drop your slate and break it. We'll get you another one."

"But you told me to be careful and I wasn't." Ruby played with the kitten's pointed ears.

Marigold tugged one of Ruby's pigtails. "I know. But it was an accident."

"But what if Uncle Gordon has an accident?"

He'll deserve it. Marigold asked for immediate forgiveness for such an uncharitable thought. She didn't need to concern herself about him except where his actions affected the girls.

"What does breaking your slate have to do with your uncle having an accident?" Marigold asked.

Ruby shook her head and didn't answer. She probably didn't know any more than Marigold did. Yet somewhere in the child's head, she connected the two.

Ruby could be a little naughty. Beryl might have a rough

tongue on her, but she never got herself dirty, did all her lessons with care and precision, and did what she was told. Ruby, on the other hand, got restless and fidgeted, didn't always obey, and got dirty just looking at the yard. She was a sweet and precious child, though. So was Beryl. How Gordon Chambers could dismiss them—

Marigold waited for his footfalls to grow silent on the steps then the upper floor, before she slipped down the hallway to the back stairs and on up to the nursery wing at the rear of the house. In the morning she could reassure the girls that their uncle was all right.

⁂

Except, in the morning, because she'd waited up half the night, Marigold didn't wake up. Two hours past her usual waking time, she roused to the girls giggling in the schoolroom and the smell of coffee. Snatching up her dressing gown, she stumbled through the doorway.

Breakfast lay spread out on the worktable. Her breakfast of toast, eggs, coffee, and an apple.

"Mrs. Cromwell helped us," Ruby announced.

"Uncle Gordon thought you might be ill." Beryl tilted her head to one side and inspected Marigold's face. "Do you have a cold? Your eyes are kind of puffy."

"Not enough sleep." Marigold hugged the girls. "And look at the two of you all dressed. Did Mrs. Cromwell help you?"

"We helped ourselves." Beryl picked up the coffeepot. "I'll pour. It's too hot for babies like Ruby."

"I'm not a baby."

"You cry like one." Beryl sent a jet of dark brown liquid arcing into the cup as though she did it every day.

"Very good." Marigold applauded.

"I buttered your toast." Ruby held up the plate—and sent eggs sliding down the front of her pinafore.

"You are such a slob!" Beryl cried.

"I didn't mean to." Ruby's eyes grew huge with tears.

"I told you to leave it—"

"You leave it, Beryl." Marigold took the plate from Ruby before any more harm occurred. "Ruby, you need to be more careful, you know that. And, Beryl, don't ever call your sister names again."

"She needs to read the Bible about love," Ruby declared.

Marigold managed not to smile. "And you need to read about forgiveness."

Her own words sent a stab of pain through her conscience. Ruby wasn't the only one who needed to read about forgiving one another. Marigold had a lot of people to forgive—Gordon, Lucian, the young lady who had accepted Lucian's advances....

"After I eat this delicious breakfast," Marigold said, "we'll go outside and read, all right?"

"Uncle Gordon went down to the beach," Beryl announced. "I want to go. We never go with you."

"It's too crowded right now." Marigold grimaced over the notion of keeping track of the girls amid the hundreds, perhaps thousands, of people on holiday.

"Then let's go to the lighthouse," Beryl persisted. "You said we could go."

"So I did." Marigold perched on her chair and picked up the coffee cup. "Ruby, change into a clean pinafore and fetch your bonnets. I'll be ready in a trice."

She was, wearing one of her cotton day dresses instead of the ugly gray things. The lighthouse was one of their favorite places. As little as she was, Ruby managed all the steps to the top then stood in awe of the panorama of sky and sea spread out below.

On top of the world like that, Marigold gloried in the beauty of the Lord's creation and managed to push thoughts of Lucian and the upcoming humiliation of her sister's wedding aside. Change seemed possible amid light and beauty. Lucian would see her and remember that he made a promise to her. Despite the harsh words they had exchanged over the back gate, they would mend their fences at the wedding.

She supposed she should mend her fences with her

employer, but he seemed preoccupied with ledgers and sailing and business meetings. She supposed she should be pleased that he seemed to be making friends with gentlemen in Cape May. Perhaps they would convince him to stay. Yet the more time he spent with others, the less he spent with his nieces, and that she couldn't abide. Her conscience pricked her a bit over that last. She should care about Gordon leaving for the girls' sake, not her own. They needed him, if they couldn't have her.

She supposed something rang falsely in that thought, too, but found herself too preoccupied about the upcoming party to think about it. Gordon didn't know she was invited, and she didn't want to tell him. He might forbid her to go, and she didn't want another reason to find him annoying.

Sometimes she found his presence in the house an irritation. She no longer felt free to play. The Chamberses had asked her to play, but Gordon closed the library door every time his nieces began work on their scales and simple melodies. Marigold didn't know if their beginner efforts bothered him, or if he didn't appreciate music. She didn't want to find out, so she avoided one of her pleasures in life—playing the piano.

One more way he had harmed her life.

"I should play in the hope it annoys him," she grumbled as she sorted through music. "Something loud and obtrusive."

No, no, she shouldn't think that way. God wouldn't want her to be mean.

"But, God, I can't forgive him for the harm his actions have caused me. What if Lucian is seriously attached to this niece of Mrs. Morris? What if—"

She made herself think of the flashes of pain she'd seen on Gordon's face when the past came up through conversation, a photograph, or an old landmark. He might have good reason for staying away, and she should have compassion.

But to go home without a fiancé stung without having yet done it.

She managed not to think about Lucian when teaching the girls, when reading, when concentrating on her anger with Gordon Chambers. Dressing for a dinner party, the first one she'd dressed for since the Chambers' deaths. Her thoughts turned to the one her parents held to announce her engagement to Lucian.

Thirty people had been present, and she'd embarrassed her sister, who was not yet engaged, despite being two years older. Rose and Marigold had argued bitterly afterward, Rose in tears, Marigold angry with herself and unable to change anything—without humiliating herself. When she couldn't bring herself to apologize because every time she looked at the goldfinch residing on her dressing table the words stuck in her throat, Father had sent her into service with the Chamberses, his business associates.

If Father hadn't done that, Lucian wouldn't have betrayed her with some distant Grassick cousin.

Surely Marigold could change that. Surely marriage to her would benefit him more than to a girl he couldn't know well, since he'd only worked at the glassworks for a few months. If Father. . .

But Lucian thought Father wanted an excuse to send her away, keep her isolated from him until he moved south to Salem County. Whoever was right, Marigold faced questions and sympathy and the pain of seeing her sister marry first.

She mustn't cry. Crying would make her eyes red, which would not look at all attractive. And Marigold wanted to look attractive. For no good reason other than feminine vanity, she wanted Gordon Chambers to faint with shock when he saw her walk into the Morrises' parlor.

Except he wasn't in the parlor when Marigold arrived. A dozen other people were, including the bespectacled Mr. Phillips, the Chamberses' attorney. He raised his eyebrows at Marigold in her blue silk gown, as did a few others who recognized her, but when Mrs. Morris introduced her as "a friend from home," people treated her like the guest she was, out of politeness to the Morrises, if nothing else.

Mr. Phillips gravitated to her side and brought her a glass of lemonade, then offered to escort her into dinner, then asked about her family.

"You know," Marigold said.

"Of course. I wouldn't have let you and the old housekeeper remain in that house alone with the children without looking into your background. You could have stolen all the silver and left the children on their own."

"I'm happy to know someone was looking out for them." Marigold curled her lip. "Unlike—ah, and here he is."

Gordon, looking rather splendid in a black broadcloth suit and shimmering white shirt, strode into the parlor and straight up to Mrs. Morris. Only the low rumble of his voice reached Marigold's ears, but she guessed what he was saying—apologies for being late.

"He had to buy a new suit," Phillips murmured.

Marigold glanced at the attorney in time to see his upper lip curl.

"You don't like him," she whispered.

He shook his head. "He was irresponsible for taking so long to get here and irresponsible for wanting to leave again. But my mother tells me I shouldn't be so hard on him. He had reason for wanting to leave Cape May."

Marigold started to ask what, realized it was gossip, and compressed her lips. If Gordon wanted her to know, he would tell her. She would not lower herself to asking.

"You are such a fine girl." Phillips took her hand in his and tucked it into the crook of his elbow. "You won't talk about your employer."

"No, sir."

"But you don't like him." Phillips started to lead her across the room.

Her skirt brushed against the scented geraniums trailing their velvety leaves from pots along the baseboard. Their lemony freshness scented the air, mingling with hair pomades and perfume. Perhaps she should see about obtaining some geraniums for the Chambers—

"You don't need to acknowledge that," Phillips was saying. "Your eyes give you away."

"Then I should keep them downcast, if they're conveying those kinds of messages."

She did dislike him. She had every reason to. He was inconsiderate and selfish. Just look how late he'd been to a party.

"Where are you taking me?" she asked the attorney.

"To meet the town's newest bachelor." Phillips laughed.

It couldn't be avoided. With only a dozen guests, Gordon would notice her sooner than later.

He noticed her when she and Phillips were still a half dozen feet away. His root beer–colored eyes widened enough for her to catch the golden lights in them.

"Mr. Chambers," Phillips called, "let me present Miss Marigold McCorkle."

"We've met." Gordon's bow was stiff, his expression too blank.

Marigold almost felt sorry for him. Almost. Mostly, she wanted to laugh.

She dropped him a curtsy. "Yes, indeed we have, Mr. Chambers. Wasn't it kind of the Morrises to invite both of us?"

"Very. . .democratic of them." Gordon glanced to Phillips. "Things have changed since I was here last."

"Not all that much," Phillips began.

Before he could elaborate, Mrs. Morris invited everyone to move to the dining room.

Gordon sat at the far end of the long table from Marigold. She sat next to Mrs. Morris on one side and Mr. Phillips on the other. Both kept her entertained. The food slid past her palate on a variety of textures, spices, and categories— poultry, fish, beef; consommé, creamed vegetables, salad; trifle, cake, chocolates. She'd forgotten that life at the Chambers household had grown austere in comparison. They had enough to eat, but it was plain, unimaginative, prepared by an excellent cook of everyday dishes. The chef had gone with the other servants. By the time Mrs. Morris led the ladies from the dining room to freshen up in the upstairs chambers, Marigold decided she preferred simple meals on a daily basis. Her corset felt like it was about to cut her in half if she so much as breathed too deeply.

She felt rather unwell and out of place among women who hired nurserymaids. They didn't entertain them.

"I should leave," she whispered to Mrs. Morris. "Before the men come in. I shouldn't have come."

Mrs. Morris looked pensive for a moment. "Do you truly care what Mr. Chambers thinks of you being here?"

"He wasn't happy to see me here. I shouldn't have come."

She'd come to tweak his nose, to annoy him. It was an unwise decision.

"I don't want him to know who I am," she explained.

"But he needs to, child. You need to go home."

Marigold's overly full stomach dropped to the bottom of her belly. "Is that why you invited me? You want Mr. Chambers to realize I shouldn't be working for him and dismiss me?"

Even before Mrs. Morris answered in the affirmative, Marigold knew the old family friend had betrayed her.

❧

Gordon wasn't annoyed so much as confused by Marigold's presence at the Morrises'. Before he'd left Cape May, he'd learned in no uncertain terms that those who employed did not fraternize with those they employed. America might be the land of opportunity, but that meant that servants could become employers, if they chose. He hadn't accepted that as a youth, who saw a damsel in distress, a maidservant damsel, and charged to the rescue—and caused trouble.

He always caused trouble when he took the time to care about someone.

Gordon didn't think social mores had changed in Cape

May over the past dozen years, yet Marigold stood chattering away with the attorney, dressed in a gown every bit as pretty and fine as those of the other women in the room, and being treated like a special guest. No wonder she didn't care what she said to him, if she had friends like the Morrises.

And why would a nurserymaid have friends like the Morrises? It had to be more than the explanation of her grandmother working for Paul Morris's family decades ago.

Gordon intended to ask her the first opportunity he received. He intended to walk her home. It was only half a block, so he didn't know how much of an answer he would receive, but he would invoke his authority over her as her employer.

The notion unsettled him. He'd never been anyone's employer. He didn't like being anyone's employer. He never rebuked Marigold for her bold speech because he'd lived in the West too long to remember that things were different in the East.

So he would ask Mr. Morris.

Gordon opened his mouth to pose the question, but music began to drift from the parlor, a piano played with a light and skillful touch.

"Ah," Mr. Morris said with a satisfied smile, "my wife has persuaded Marigold to play for us."

Gordon followed the other men into the room, then stood in the doorway and stared regardless of the rudeness of doing so. Marigold perched on the stool, her gown billowing around her, her hair subdued to a rich auburn in the gaslight. She held her back straight, but not rigid, and music flowed from her fingertips as though it came directly from her instead of the instrument.

In that moment, he understood why he endured her boldness. He knew why he smiled even when she made him angry.

He was fast on his way to falling in love with her.

The realization set his resolve to end matters that night.

He couldn't have her under his roof under the circumstances. He couldn't risk hurting her. If it meant he had to take the first applicant who approached the door, he would see Marigold gone the following day. Women never failed to complicate his life beyond patience. He was certain God had shown him he should be alone. How else had he eluded the clutches of dozens of females in the past dozen years? God had protected him and kept directing him onward, to where few people lived, especially not females, with their troubles.

And their deceptions.

He found himself seated on a sofa with Mrs. Morris while he listened to Marigold play. Most people talked. Gordon listened, enthralled, enchanted, sick with a knot forming in his middle.

"Who is she?" he asked at last.

"Marigold McCorkle." Mrs. Morris smiled. "Do you know the story of the goldfinch bottle?"

"I don't think so. Should I have?"

"Perhaps not. It's a tale of faithfulness and giving up what's too important to us for our hearts to serve God." Mrs. Morris settled back against the hard, pink and white–striped cushions. "About ninety years ago, a young Scots glassblower made a goldfinch bottle for his fiancée. That man was Colin Grassick, and he married the owner of the glassworks that employed him."

"Grassick." A bell rang in Gordon's head. "Your husband's sister's married to a Grassick."

"Yes, Colin Grassick's grandson. Because of youthful indiscretions, he lost the goldfinch. It was starting to be passed on to the eldest son."

Gordon rested his elbow on the arm of the sofa and hoped the warmth of the room and his full stomach wouldn't send him to sleep over a tale he didn't understand why he should know.

"My husband's sister helped Daire Grassick find the goldfinch," Mrs. Morris continued, "and throughout it all, Daire learned that it was just too important to him and his family, so he gave it to the son of the Morrises' maid. That gift and help from the Grassicks gave the McCorkles the push they needed to better their lives. They're quite prosperous, and both of their daughters have graduated from Vassar."

Gordon jerked upright. "Marigold? I mean, Miss McCorkle?"

Mrs. Morris smiled and nodded. "And now she's inherited the goldfinch. At least she did. There weren't any males in her generation, so her father decided it would go to the first daughter to marry."

"Miss McCorkle is getting married?" Gordon felt like the fish from dinner had come alive and begun to swim about in his belly at this news.

"Not any longer. When you took so long to arrive, her fiancé broke off the engagement."

nine

Marigold glanced from Gordon's proffered arm to her gloved hand to the tips of her white shoes peeking from beneath the bottom ruffle on her gown. "I'm quite all right walking on my own, thank you."

"A gentleman offers a lady his arm when escorting her, Miss McCorkle." Gordon's tone was as grim as his expression.

Marigold let her gaze stray to Mrs. Morris. The older lady smiled and nodded.

Marigold ground her teeth and rested her fingertips on the sleeve of Gordon's coat.

She'd taken Mr. Phillips' arm without a moment's hesitation, and he'd been nearly a stranger until that night. She knew Gordon Chambers. She should welcome his courtesy for the half-block stroll home.

Or perhaps she welcomed it too much. She was supposed to be in mourning for her lost fiancé, not liking the feel of the strong arm beneath her hand. Her heart was supposed to be breaking, not her person tingling, as though she anticipated a run straight across hot sand to dive into cold water.

Her face stiff, as though she'd spent too much time in frigid temperatures, Marigold bade her host and hostess good night and allowed Gordon to lead her from the house. To call his pace leisurely would exaggerate the speed. He crept down the sidewalk like a man three times his age. And he said nothing past the first house. Quiet filled the night, save for the distant rumble of carriage wheels and the whisper of the ocean breeze through the trees.

Wanting to burst into raucous singing, Marigold tossed out a question in front of the second house they passed. "So what did Mrs. Morris tell you about me?"

"Why," he demanded, as he stopped and faced her, "didn't you tell me what you lost by staying with my nieces when I delayed so long getting here?"

"Why did you take so long getting here?"

"That doesn't concern you."

"Apparently it does, since you just asked me why I didn't tell you about my canceled wedding."

"I—" He set his mouth in a thin line, then sighed. "You're right. I caused the difficulty. That gives you a measure of a right to know. But. . .it's difficult."

She said nothing. She didn't move.

That one corner of his mouth twitched. "You're stubborn, aren't you?"

She remained still.

"I honestly didn't get the telegram for nearly a month. Then. . ." He looked away. "I did have some business matters to settle before I left New Mexico, but, yes, mostly it was because my brother's death grieved me, and I couldn't face the idea of coming back here, facing this place without him. Not particularly manly of me, is it?"

"I think that took about as much courage as a man can have to admit."

She thought a great deal more, too. Nothing she would share with him—her shame for being so annoyed with him, her softening heart toward him. Too softening.

She needed to be away, to be home with her family, seeing Lucian when he returned for visits, mending matters, restoring her relationships. She couldn't begin to have a regard for a man who wanted nothing more than to abandon people he should love.

Yet now she understood he just might have a reason.

"We can't undo the past," she said. "So no sense in worrying over it."

"I feel responsible for the damage I caused you with my

thoughtlessness. I didn't think. . . . I didn't realize. . . ."

"If Lucian's love is so weak," Marigold said with more bravado than she felt, "he isn't—I'm better off. . . ." She blinked to clear her vision. "What's done is done."

"Perhaps not. You said you were to be in your sister's wedding. Are you not going home for it within the week?"

"Yes, but I don't know how you would manage, you and Mrs. Cromwell. Ruby's so worried lately, whenever anyone leaves her, and if I go home. . ." She turned away and folded her arms across her middle to hold in a sudden stab of pain that bore no resemblance to physical discomfort.

Her discomfort lay in her heart, in her spirit, in her soul.

"You can't stay here just because Ruby doesn't want you to go away, Miss McCorkle."

Miss McCorkle. Somehow his using her surname instead of "Miss Marigold" hurt. Though only a foot of warm night air swirled between them, it felt like a wall, or a hurricane blowing her out of Cape May.

"You can't stay." Gordon's voice hardened. "I cannot continue to have a lady from your family acting as my nieces' nurserymaid."

"You're—you're dismissing me?" Marigold's eyes widened. "You're not just telling me to go home for my sister's wedding? You're telling me to go home—forever?"

Poultry and pie warred in her belly. Her throat burned. In a moment she was going to be sick right there in front of an elegant mansion.

She swallowed and plunged on. "You take three months to get here. You give no explanation as to why. You make me postpone my wedding until my fiancé gives up on me, until my charges are convinced I am the only constant left in their lives, until I have to bear the shame of—you're dismissing me because I'm not in need of this position? Why you, you—"

He laid his forefinger across her lips. "Careful, or you'll give me more cause to dismiss you."

For a full minute, they stood motionless in the center of the sidewalk, his finger burning against her mouth, her heart racing. Her lips moved; she thought to protest. She realized she had just kissed his hand. She jerked away and spun on her heel. Skirts crushed between her shaking fingers, she ran away from him. Her heels clattered on the sidewalk. Her breath rasped in her throat, from panting or sobs she neither knew nor cared. Getting away was what mattered, far away, secluded in her room, where she could cry all she liked and no one would have to know.

She not only had to face the humiliation of going home to see her sister married, she had to face seeing her unfaithful fiancé with another woman, face the moment when she would be expected to hand the goldfinch over to her sister, and now to confess she had been dismissed from her position because her family had pulled themselves out of poverty— because she was arrogant and insolent to her employer.

Because she'd kissed his hand.

Surely dying was easier than enduring such humiliation.

She didn't reach her room before the floodgates opened and tears spilled down her face. Sobbing, she dropped onto a chair in the kitchen and rested her head on her folded arms. Life had been going so well for her. She had graduated from college; she, a female, had a better education than anyone in her family. She was engaged to a handsome and talented man, engaged before her sister. She would receive the goldfinch to pass along to her children. Yes, Father had sent her into service, but she loved the girls and the Chambers family had told her again and again she was indispensable. When Gerald and Katherine Chambers died, Mrs. Cromwell begged Marigold to stay. The lawyer and banker sent her letters begging her to stay. She was needed, important.

Now she was nothing but a passably pretty spinster with no prospects.

Her gut tightened. Her chest tightened. She felt as though

someone had lit Independence Day fireworks inside her, and they were about to blow up.

She wanted to rush upstairs and start packing. If she slipped away early enough, she could catch the train without seeing Gordon Chambers another time. He could send her wages to her. Perhaps, if she went quietly, he would write her a reference so she could find other work, perhaps work that would take her west to someplace out of the way.

Like Gordon Chambers wanted?

For the first time since hearing of the prodigal Chambers brother, Marigold understood the lure of open spaces without man to interfere in one's life. It would be refreshing, not in the least judgmental—

Lonely.

The fireworks exploded, leaving Marigold hollow inside; a gaping wound of loneliness filled in the space where her heart had been at the notion of going day after day without people around her to love and need her. She was so fond of the girls.

She loved the girls so much; she couldn't run away from them. She couldn't leave them at all. Yes, she had to go to her sister's wedding, endure the stares, the whispers, the pitying glances, but she must return, must persuade Gordon that he couldn't do without her.

She must make herself indispensable yet again.

During a restless night, in which she slept little and paced her room a great deal, she figured out a small action she could take to help him.

He needed to be certain that Lawrence Randall was honest, despite that single warning by the former employee. He had good reason to wonder. Dennis Tripp was a Christian man. Quiet and devout, he never missed church, praised God for having a purpose even after he lost his position, always helped those in need despite his own meager income.

She would take a page from his book, so to speak, and

would go over the ledgers she'd seen on Gordon's desk. He might have been a supercargo for a merchantman, but Marigold could wave her degree and course work in math from Vassar and all the accounting she had done for her father's business interests.

Before dawn on Monday morning, she washed, dressed, and slipped downstairs. With a cup of tea at her elbow, she began to go through the ledgers. The oldest one lay open on Gordon's desk. A glance said it was all right and that his calculations added up with the numbers in the book. Marigold decided to recheck his calculations. And he was correct. Everything added up. The only odd thing she noticed, something Gordon couldn't know, was a number of names of employees she didn't recognize. Not that she would know everyone in Cape May with so many people coming to the town for the summer work. Still, apparently Dennis Tripp wasn't the only employee who had lost his position soon after Gerald Chambers' death. She should point this out to Gordon: How many names had been rubbed out and added in elsewhere so that following the thread of who worked when grew bewildering, even for her. First, she would look into it herself.

She rose from the desk, slipped upstairs to ensure that the girls still slept and to collect her hat, then left the house. The back gate led her into the alley. From there, she cut through other backstreets to keep her off the boardwalk as long as possible. In minutes, she stood outside the boathouse ready to pounce upon—or at the least, enter with—the first employee to reach the office and unlock the door.

She leaned against the portal and studied the boats bobbing on the ebb tide. Mist blurred their outlines, making them look like crafts floating out of dreams. Despite the warmth of the morning, Marigold shivered. On just such a day, the Chamberses went for a sail and returned on the tide after a sudden, violent storm, their boat wrecked, their bodies battered and bruised.

Marigold prayed the fog didn't portend another storm but merely a rain shower later that might break the stale humidity of the air. If the fog continued, the excursions would be canceled and the boathouse empty of all but employees.

And if Dennis Tripp was correct, she could be in danger.

"Ha," Marigold laughed aloud. She was being fanciful, ridiculous. Nonetheless, she wondered if she should leave, point out the changed employees to Gordon, and go about the business for which she had been hired—tending to the girls.

Hands tucked under her arms, she turned from the doorway. A shadow moved across the sand, his features indistinct in the murky light. He headed straight for the office. Keys already jingled in his hand. She couldn't leave without him seeing her. So she waited, waited until he drew near enough for her to recognize him as one of the clerks. Good. Mr. Randall would be harder to persuade.

"I've come to find out about the influx of new employees here—for Mr. Chambers, of course." She spoke a little too loudly, quickly, to take the man by surprise. "You have records on these men, of course."

He jumped and dropped the keys.

Marigold retrieved them. "Allow me, sir." She fitted the brass key into the lock. It turned as though recently oiled—without sound or hitch.

"Miss, I can't allow you—" The clerk snatched for the keys.

"Of course you can." Marigold pushed open the door. "I'm on an errand for Mr. Chambers, the owner." She scanned the room that never seemed to change. Dusty ledgers, inkstand desks, boxes of tickets. "Where can I find the most recent list of employees and when it changed?"

"You can't until Mr. Randall returns." The clerk wrung his hands. "Please, no one is supposed to be in here. I could lose my position."

"I won't tell, if you don't. Where's Mr. Randall?"

"Sleeping, like decent folks still are."

Marigold raised her eyebrows. "Are you saying you're not decent? If so, perhaps Mr. Chambers shouldn't employ you."

"Of course I'm decent." The clerk's flush glowed even in the dim light. "I am at work, as some of us should be."

"I'm working, too." Marigold smiled. "For Mr. Chambers. Those lists, please."

She tucked the keys into her pocket and held out her hand.

"Miss, er—I don't know of any lists or change of employees, Miss McCorkle."

"Of course you do, Mr. Pollock. You've worked here for twenty years, I understand. Where are the lists? Or don't you keep clear records of who works here and who doesn't?"

"Of course we have clear records of employees. They're in Mr. Randall's office. So you see, I can't get them for you."

"Huh." Marigold sidled past him and approached Randall's office door.

Pollock scampered behind. "You cannot—"

Marigold twisted the knob. Locked. She drew out the keys. Pollock snatched for them.

"You wouldn't harm a lady, would you, Mr. Pollock?"

"You're a maid, not a lady."

"Mr. Chambers would disagree with you on that score." She fitted another key into the lock. Nothing. She tried a third key.

Click.

"Very good." She pushed open the door.

Air smelling of tobacco and spirits smacked her in the face. She wrinkled her nose and headed for the dim shadow of the desk. Six books lay upon it.

Mr. Pollock charged forward and set himself between Marigold and the desk. "You cannot. We could both lose our positions."

"I have nothing to lose, so do, please, step aside." She strode around him, certain he wouldn't outright lay hands on her.

"And I'll ensure that if Mr. Randall dismisses you that Mr. Chambers hires you back, unless you're up to skulduggery here, of course."

"Nothing of the kind, Miss McCorkle."

The clerk's lower lip stuck out and quivered like a child's.

Marigold nearly backed down, but the man's odd actions set the hairs on the back of her neck to prickling. She slipped around the desk and flipped open the top ledger at random, then she ruffled through some pages while the clerk spluttered and backed away. It didn't look the same as the ones in Gordon's office. It was far neater.

She snatched up both stacks of books. "Good day, Mr. Pollock. If Mr. Randall has any questions, he can come to the Chambers house." Before the man decided to tackle her for the heavy volumes, Marigold trotted out the door.

"Miss," Pollock called after her. "The keys."

"Send someone for them," she shouted back. "My hands are full."

By the time she was halfway back to the Chambers house, her conscience pricked her as badly as her hackles. She shouldn't have taken advantage of the old man, if he was innocent of any wrongdoing. He probably did need his position, and Randall was likely to dismiss him. Somehow, though, she would make things right. Gordon would make things right. He was the owner of the business, not Lawrence Randall. As for the keys, Pollock wouldn't need them for a while. She would take them back later.

Despite telling herself nothing permanently bad would happen from her actions, she lugged her burden with a heavy heart. Perhaps this wasn't the kind of "indispensable" Gordon would like. Perhaps he would prefer to see to matters himself.

Except he hadn't seen to them very well himself.

Mouth set, mind prepared for any kind of argument from Gordon Chambers, Marigold strode into the house.

Mrs. Cromwell stood at the stove frying eggs. She gasped

at sight of Marigold. "What are you doing with those books this early and in this fog?"

"I got them for Mr. Chambers." Marigold continued through the kitchen and into the library.

To her relief, Gordon was nowhere around. She set the ledgers on the desk then raced upstairs. Though beginning to stir, the girls still slept. Marigold removed her hat and washed dust from the ledgers off her hands before she returned to the girls' room and touched their shoulders to wake them up.

"No walk today," she explained. "It's too foggy and may rain soon."

"Can we draw pictures?" Ruby asked.

"May we? Yes."

"Big ones." Beryl sat up, rubbing her eyes. "I want to draw big pictures if we can't go outside."

So Marigold worked out how they could create large pictures. After the girls ate breakfast, she glued several sheets of drawing paper together and hung them on the schoolroom wall low enough for Ruby to reach the top edge. Armed with colored chalks, the girls set to work. Marigold slipped downstairs in time to find Gordon entering the library. She paused in the doorway, not certain if she should tell him about the ledgers or let him discover them himself.

He could hardly miss them. They took up half the desk. Still, he didn't go to the desk immediately. He drew back the draperies from the windows to reveal rain-streaked glass. For a moment, he bowed his head, his shoulders slumped. Not a good time to intrude on his privacy.

Marigold started to turn away.

"Wait!" he called to her.

She waited.

"Where are the girls?" he asked.

"In the schoolroom, drawing."

"They're all right alone?"

Marigold laughed. "Of course. They're six and nine years

old, not six and nine months old."

"I didn't know. . ." He sighed. "Please come in."

Slowly, Marigold faced him. His eyes looked shadowed. Lines radiated from the corners of his mouth, and his jaw sported a lump of bunched muscle.

So he hadn't been sleeping any better than she had.

"Miss McCorkle. Please sit down. We need to talk about replacing you."

Marigold remained standing. "I won't talk about replacing me. If you insist on doing so, then you will do so, but you've already told me to go, so I have nothing to lose by disobeying you."

He narrowed his eyes. "I feel like a fool for not realizing all along you weren't a regular serving girl. You have too much pride."

"That's precisely why I'm a serving girl. My father thought I needed to be humbled a bit."

"It didn't work, apparently," came his dry response.

A reluctant smile tugged at her lips. "Not particularly. But right now—" Her throat closed. Her eyes blurred.

"Are you all right?" He took a step toward her.

She nodded.

"Good." He strolled across the room and started around the desk. "After your sister's wedding—what's this?" He looked down at the ledgers.

"The ledgers Mr. Randall should have given you."

Marigold's tone held a hard edge that kept the tears at bay. "You didn't notice because you started with the oldest ones, but these are newer."

Gordon stared at her. "Dare I ask how you got these?"

"I walked in and took them. It's not Mr. Pollock's fault if Randall dismisses him."

"I see." He flipped open the first book. "Why did you bring these?"

"You need them. If Mr. Tripp is telling lies about the

business, then he needs to be proven wrong, or he'll ruin it. If Mr. Randall is in the wrong, then he needs to be stopped."

"Yes, that's why I'm going through the books, but why did you. . .involve yourself?"

"I like numbers." She squared her shoulders. "I worked for my father for years and often found errors—" She lowered her gaze. "I'm boasting, aren't I?"

"Yes." He coughed. "And it may have gotten you into a pickle. If you like numbers so much, then perhaps you should be the one going through the ledgers, not I."

"I already have. The names of employees—skippers on the boats, deckhands, and so on—confused me, so I got these from Randall."

"He gave them to you?" Gordon looked dubious.

Marigold shrugged. "No one stopped me from taking them."

"I see." He tightened the corners of his lips, but one corner twitched suspiciously. "You don't want to continue with dusty old books, though."

"It's such a rainy day, and the temperature is dropping, so going through books is a perfect way to pass the time when the girls don't need me."

"I thought females read novels on cold, rainy days."

"No, sir, I'd rather read Adam Smith."

"*Wealth of Nations*?" He shuddered. "I think I'd prefer to read a novel." He smiled.

Marigold smiled. "Let me see if the girls are all right, then I'll get to work."

The girls were happily coloring in leaves on the trees they'd drawn leaning so far over a body of water they looked about to topple into the stream at any moment.

"You should make their reflection in the water," Marigold suggested. "Now, if you need me, I'll be in the library."

The girls scarcely acknowledged her presence as they proceeded to discuss and squabble, in a friendly way, whether the trees' reflection would show in their water.

Marigold returned to the library, pulled a ledger from the stack, and settled in front of the hearth. When the air grew chilly and damp, Gordon built a fire. Mrs. Cromwell brought in hot tea and cookies. Marigold thought as she drank her tea and nibbled the cinnamon and sugar pastries. She focused on her work, seeking discrepancies. She hoped she would find them. One more way she would be indispensable. Gordon would tell her to return after the wedding. If things didn't work out with Lucian, she could tell everyone that she was needed on Cape May, needed for two orphaned girls whose uncle didn't care enough to stay among civilized people—

She stopped thinking in that direction. Numbers first. Numbers that worked out with revolting accuracy and neatness throughout the day—with one exception.

"It's odd that Leonard Pollock's name never appears in here," she told Gordon. "I know he works there. I talked to him when I took the rest of the ledgers."

"Do you recognize any of the names?" he asked.

Marigold shook her head. "I've never heard of any of these people, and you'd think that I would have after a year in Cape May. For local people, it's a small town."

"Could my brother have brought in outsiders?"

"Ye–es." Marigold began to ponder the name differences, but when Ruby called for her, she spent the rest of the afternoon helping the girls finish their drawing and then practicing the piano.

At dinnertime, she went into the kitchen and helped Mrs. Cromwell prepare the meal and set the table.

"You shouldn't be in the library alone with Mr. Gordon," the older woman admonished. "It doesn't look right."

"He hasn't been in there a great deal of the time," Marigold pointed out. "But he might be this evening."

"Then you should go up to the schoolroom."

"I'd rather keep working."

"So Mr. Gordon can leave us sooner?"

"So I can find something wrong, and he'll have to stay." The instant she spoke, Marigold wished she had bitten off her tongue rather than speak. "I mean. . . I didn't intend. . ."

"You spoke your mind." Mrs. Cromwell patted her arm. "That's all right. None of us wants him to leave these little girls."

"But you want to leave."

Mrs. Cromwell sighed. "No, I don't want to. I'll worry about them every day, if I don't pray hard for them, and even then probably will, but I need to retire, child. I'm getting too old to handle this much work, and the winters are hard on my old bones."

"I understand. My great-grandmother had to move down to Georgia a few years ago for the same reason. I miss her."

"Then you go down and visit her. Family is important."

"I know. But right now. . ." Marigold twisted the dish towel so hard it began to tear.

Not even to this dear lady could she admit that her family only reminded her of how she wasn't going to have a husband and children of her own. She was expected to stand up there with the other bridesmaids and smile and pretend she was happy for Rose.

She was, of course. She simply couldn't help thinking how awful it was going to be to have to endure others' pity, especially when her parents would expect her to hand over the goldfinch to Rose.

It's only a thing, she reminded herself. It was a piece of glass. An old and beautiful piece of glass.

With a whole lot of meaning behind it—love and constancy, sacrifice and the strength of knowing one was not alone.

But she was alone now and didn't deserve the bird. She hadn't been able to keep her fiancé interested in her. She was better off without him. He didn't have a constant heart. But her heart ached with emptiness. Where now would she find someone she could marry, so she wouldn't end up a spinster living with her parents even more years than she had already, watching Rose so happy and raising children?

A tray of hot coffee in her hands, Marigold returned to the library, to Gordon Chambers, a man who needed to learn he shouldn't be alone.

ten

Gordon didn't know how to tell Marigold to stop working on the ledgers. The grandfather clock in the foyer had long since chimed eleven o'clock. Mrs. Cromwell nodded in the chair she had settled by the door so she could chaperone. And Gordon could scarcely see numbers for the grit in his eyes.

Marigold, on the other hand, chewed on the end of a pencil while working out numbers on one of several sheets of paper, her face intent behind curls that had escaped their pins hours ago. She seemed impervious to the hour or the fact that she'd been working over the books for three hours without so much as moving from her chair.

More loudly than necessary, Gordon rose, stretched, and gathered up the tray of hot chocolate Mrs. Cromwell had made for them an hour earlier. With a flick of his finger, he sent a spoon cascading onto the marble hearth. It landed with a ring of fine silver on stone.

Marigold jumped and looked up. "Oh, yes, let me help with that." She set the books aside and reached for the spoon.

Gordon reached for the spoon.

Their heads collided.

"I think we've done this before." He rubbed his scalp.

She pressed a hand to her head. "I am so sorry. Are you all right?"

"I am. You have a great deal of padding on your head."

"I have what?" She stared at him with wide, green eyes.

He grinned despite his fatigue and did what he'd wanted to do for weeks—pull one of her curls. "Your hair cushioned the blow."

"Oh, this." She grimaced. "Do you know a hundred years

ago women cut their hair short? I think that would have been wonderfully freeing."

"I like it as it is."

He hadn't intended to say anything. He thought he considered her hair a disaster. Yet it was so vibrant, so full of energy and life—like her—he couldn't imagine her with sleek, obedient tresses.

He tucked his hands behind his back to stop himself from touching one of those silky curls again, burying his fingers in it and drawing her face to his, kissing her—

A man who wanted open space and peace didn't find himself attracted to a female who was anything but peaceful. A man who feared the harm he brought those with whom he grew close, those he loved, didn't dare take a wife, start a family.

Care for his orphaned nieces.

Yet leaving seemed more difficult with every person he met, every moment he spent with the girls, every time he looked at Marigold.

He scrambled to his feet. "It's late. Mrs. Cromwell needs her rest, even if you don't."

"Of course." She masked it quickly, but he caught the flash of hurt on her face. "I can finish up this work in the next two days, before I leave." She bowed her head and scrambled to her feet. "I am sorry, Mrs. Cromwell. Why don't you stay in bed and sleep late tomorrow? I'll make breakfast."

"Can you make a decent breakfast, too?" Gordon asked.

"Of course." Marigold picked up the serving tray and trotted from the room.

Gordon went to the housekeeper and took her hands. "Let me help you up, madam."

"Watch out for that young lady." She smiled as she stood, her joints popping. "She's trying to impress you for a reason."

"She knows better than to set her cap for me. She just doesn't want to go home without a fiancé. Rather humiliating, I'd think."

"Even more so if you knew what her sister looks like."

"Pretty?"

"Plain as skim milk, but she has the sweetest nature a body can possess this side of heaven. And her fiancé is one of the best-looking young men these old eyes have ever seen." She chuckled.

Gordon frowned. "You know the family?"

"Her sister came down to introduce Marigold to her fiancé last September."

"So my brother knew Marigold—I mean, Miss McCorkle—when he hired her?"

"Not Marigold, but her father."

"Why didn't you tell me?"

"Marigold asked me not to." Mrs. Cromwell stifled a yawn. "As to why Gerald hired her, you'll have to ask her."

No, he didn't. The less he knew of her the better. In fact, avoiding her until she departed would be an excellent idea.

An idea he carried out over the next two days. He knew she worked on the ledgers when not with the girls, so he stayed away. He went fishing one day and climbed to the top of the lighthouse another morning. One day he simply walked, pausing at the derelict structure that had been a man's dream of entertainment—the wood and tin elephant. Standing seventy feet high, it had allowed people to climb inside the huge legs and sit down to enjoy ice cream. One could climb to the top and look out to sea. Now it was an eyesore, a blot on the lovely city, and someone had been commissioned to tear it down.

He'd gained his love for being alone at the top of that elephant. He would pay a dime for the privilege of standing on the elephant's back, above most people, and gaze out to sea, dreaming of what lay beyond the horizon.

He'd taken Louisa there once on her afternoon off. She'd been so pretty; even her plain dress looked finer than those of the society ladies around them. Was she still pretty, or had those fine looks and that sweet nature gotten her further in life? She'd wanted so much more than she had, and he—

"Why are you staring at that, Uncle Gordon?" Ruby asked beside him.

Gordon glanced down. If they'd greeted him, he hadn't heard. "I liked to climb up there when I was a young man."

"It's ugly," Beryl pronounced. "Why would you want to climb it?"

"It wasn't ugly then. Well. . ." He grinned. "I suppose it was, but it has steps inside, and one can see a long way from the top. There was even an ice cream parlor inside."

"I wish there was now." Ruby stuck her fingers in her mouth. In silence, Marigold tugged them out again. She looked tired, with shadows beneath her eyes and a pallor to her skin.

"Isn't it late in the day for one of your walks?" he asked.

"We need new shoes," Ruby said.

"I need new shoes." Beryl grimaced at her tiny black boots. "These are getting too small, but Ruby can wear them. They're hardly worn at all."

"I want new shoes, not your old ones. Mommy doesn't make me have old shoes."

"Mommy isn't here anymore, and Miss Marigold likes to practice economies." Beryl cast Marigold an approving glance. "We probably aren't as rich as we used to be."

"You are quite well off," Gordon said, "but that doesn't mean you should spend irresponsibly. There are a lot of people in this world who need things."

"Like Miss Marigold." Ruby stuck her fingers in her mouth then took them out again before continuing. "She needs a husband."

"I think it's time to go." Marigold clasped Ruby's hand. "Come along, Beryl."

The girls protested. Gordon told them to go. Marigold didn't look at him.

Go, indeed. Having her around, knowing she was in his house under what amounted to false pretenses, made him too uncomfortable.

He stayed away for several more hours, wandering along the beach. When the sun began to vanish behind the houses, he returned via the backstreets.

And found his nieces playing with the kitten in the yard.

"Shouldn't you be ready for bed by now?" he asked.

"Miss Marigold sent us outside to play." Ruby stuck her fingers in her mouth.

Beryl gave her a reproachful look. "You and the cat were getting in her way while she was fixing dinner."

"Why is she fixing dinner?" Gordon glanced to the house just as a billow of smoke sailed out the back door. "Stay here," he commanded.

He raced for the house. Smoke filled the kitchen, so thick he could scarcely see. Instantly, he began to cough. The kitchen reeked of burning chicken and onions.

Covering his nose and mouth with one arm, he darted to the stove. No flames on the top, only a pan smoking enough to send signals to Philadelphia. It snapped and sizzled and glowed like metal in a forge.

He snatched up a dish towel and wrapped it around his hand. Holding his breath, he carried the smoking and hissing mess outside. "Stay out of my way, girls," he called, unable to see them through the steam rising before him.

He carried the pan to the gravel of the alley and set it down where it could do no harm, except cause a bit of stink.

"Eeew." Beryl appeared beside him, holding her nose. "That's awful. What is it?"

"Dinner, I'm afraid." Gordon spun on his heel and headed for the house. "Where's Mrs. Cromwell—and Marigold?"

Mrs. Cromwell was nowhere in sight, but now that the smoke had cleared a bit, Gordon noticed Marigold sitting at the kitchen table, her head down on her folded arms.

He touched her shoulder. "Are you all right?"

She didn't respond or budge.

"Marigold?" His heart began to race until he felt breathless. "Marigold." He shook her.

She jumped. Her head slammed back against his belt buckle. "Ouch." She rubbed the back of her head. "What did you hit me with?"

"You hit your head on me." Still feeling as though he'd run a race, Gordon backed away from her. "You fell asleep and burned dinner."

"I did?" She blinked up at him then glanced around. Her nose wrinkled. "Oh, dear. Oh, dear. Oh, dear." Rubbing her eyes, she stumbled to her feet. "So very sorry. I'll think up something else to make."

"Where's Mrs. Cromwell?" Gordon averted his gaze from the sight of Marigold's tumbled hair and sleep-misty eyes.

In that moment, she appeared too soft and pretty for his comfort.

"She's visiting her sister," Marigold said, "to try to persuade her to stay here a bit longer, so I offered to make dinner. But I was up late with the ledgers. They're almost done—and—"

"You're done with them. I shouldn't be allowing you to do my work for me."

"But I love numbers."

"Then do numbers for your father. My business affairs are my concern." Realizing his tone and words were too harsh, he added, "I am grateful for all the work you've done, Miss McCorkle, and it's past time you left for Hudson City and home. Surely your family wants you."

"Yes, but. . ." She bowed her head. "I'll go pack my things after dinner."

"You can go now. I'll take the girls to a restaurant. They're both old enough to behave in public."

"But they'll need their dresses changed and—no, I'll make dinner. I–I'm supposed to be a maidservant. And I need—" She gazed at him with pleading eyes. "I need to come back, Mr. Chambers. I can't stay home, and you need me here."

"You'll be gone for a week." Gordon made himself speak with an authoritative edge to his voice. "By the end of that time, I'll have hired someone to replace you."

"I see. Then I'll pack all my things."

If she'd cried, he might not have cared so much that his harshness hurt her. Females used tears too recklessly. He'd been duped by feminine tears as a young man, lured by the sympathy they evoked in him into being foolish and hurtful to others.

He wanted to reach out to her, assure her that he appreciated the work she'd done for him. Before he found the right words, she had slipped out of the kitchen and headed up the back stairs. Her footfalls echoed on the bare, wooden treads.

The next day, when she had taken a carriage to the train station, he still heard the echo of her flying heels beating against the steps. Each beat slammed into his heart, echoing in the hollowness there.

He wondered why he'd let her go and how he could get her back.

≈

Marigold walked into a household of organized chaos. Gifts filled every available surface in the front parlor. The aromas of roasting meats and baking cakes wafted from the kitchen, and bits of ribbon and fabric created a silky layer to the carpet of hallway and steps. From the second floor, laughter drifted like the fall of ribbon scraps. Laughter overflowing with joy. Rose, ecstatic with her future settled and her wedding in two days' time.

Her luggage resting where the driver of the carriage from the train station had left it, in a meager pile in the foyer, Marigold began to gather up ribbons as she mounted the steps toward the laughter, toward the joy, toward the acknowledgment that she was not the one to star in this performance.

Not only that, she wasn't welcome back to Cape May. Gordon had made that clear. He didn't need her. For all her sleepless nights, she couldn't reconcile the two sets of ledgers in any way that said Randall and his clerks had done anything wrong but change employees and keep a sloppy set of books.

Dennis Tripp must have been mistaken or was trying to get even with the man who had dismissed him, a fact which saddened Marigold. She'd thought Mr. Tripp was a good, Christian man, who wouldn't indulge in petty revenge.

Yet why would a man try to take revenge in a way that could so easily be proven wrong?

Simply because it couldn't easily be proven right or wrong. For all her skill as a bookkeeper, she had found no conclusive evidence of wrongdoing.

Marigold paused at the top of the steps to gather up a scrap of veiling. Bridal veiling. Rose would be so pretty behind the gauzy fabric, her freckles dimmed, her pale lashes unimportant, her hair, even more orange red than Marigold's, hidden. Her sweet smile would shine through, and Adam would only see the beautiful person Rose was inside her skin, not the plain and painfully shy girl with the ability to paint birds in such detail they looked like they would fly off the page.

Birds like the goldfinch.

Marigold swiveled on her heel to change course from her trajectory toward the laughter to plod toward her own room. It would be ready for her, aired and cleaned, as she would share it with cousins visiting from out West for the wedding. Before she announced to her sister that she was home, Marigold needed to collect the family heirloom that now belonged to Rose, the sister no one thought would marry.

The door to Marigold's room stood open. Grass green carpet shone with recent cleaning, and a window stood open to catch the breezes off the river. Scents of late roses and recently cut grass floated through the window like welcome guests at the door, the summer smells she'd grown up with, had inhaled while holding the goldfinch and dreaming of the man she would marry.

Lucian fulfilled all her childish imaginings—tall and handsome, ambitious and skilled, and professing a faith in the Lord. Now that she was home for good, perhaps she could change his mind, renew their relationship. She had no other commitments in her life. She'd loved Lucian for years, prayed for several to have him notice her among all other girls. Finally he had—until she was no longer in sight. So now that she was, though, he was in Salem County working except for a few visits home. This wedding, when he would be home for the celebration of his friend, was her only chance to convince him he'd made a mistake in breaking things off with her. He was simply piqued at her long absence, her change of plans. She would humble herself and be compliant now. But even if she were successful in restoring her love life, it was too late for her to keep the goldfinch. By rights, Rose should already have it in her room.

Marigold paused before her dressing table and lifted the goldfinch bottle from its secure resting place before the mirror. Hands shaking only a little, she held up the ornament. Afternoon sunshine gleamed in the fragile amber glass, depicting each fine detail Colin Grassick had etched in hot glass ninety years earlier, a gift for the lady he loved. His son had given it to the lady he loved, and his son would have done likewise, but he'd made mistakes as a young man and lost the goldfinch. It came into the hands of Marigold's grandfather. Daire Grassick had told her grandfather, a poor Irish immigrant, to keep the goldfinch.

For Marigold's grandfather, the bird symbolized generosity and trust. He and Daire Grassick became friends. Through that friendship, the McCorkles prospered.

To Marigold, the goldfinch symbolized how far a body could change, from her grandparents being so poor they lived in one room to her and Rose growing up in a house, which, if not a mansion, was larger than four people needed, and attending private schools and college. She and Lucian should be living in a fine house in Salem County near the glassworks, where she would have displayed the goldfinch on the parlor mantel, letting everyone know how she was connected to the Grassicks from many years back. The Grassicks, after all, displayed photographs of the goldfinch in their house and the glassworks. She, Marigold McCorkle—

She located the special box for the goldfinch and tucked the glass bird into its layers of cotton wool. She'd been so proud of her family for owning this bit of glass that she wanted to be the one to carry it on to her own children.

Maybe if she could win Lucian back, no one would expect her to give up the glass. After all, she'd postponed her wedding for a noble cause. But she would make the gesture of giving it to Rose. Their parents would be proud of their elder daughter for understanding the new tradition they began when they'd only produced daughters.

Smile affixed to her face, Marigold held the box aloft like a holy grail and headed down the corridor to Rose's room, from which the laughter and chatter rippled like reflected sunlight on waves.

It ceased the instant Marigold appeared in the doorway. Rose, three of her friends, and Momma swung away from a pile of beautiful dresses and undergarments spread across the bed. Rose's trousseau, of course. No, the dresses were all alike. They must be bridesmaid dresses.

Marigold's head lightened. She clutched at the door frame. Of course she was in the wedding. Rose's sister was expected to stand up with her. Stand up in front of everyone, a bridesmaid instead of a bride.

"When did you get home?" Momma asked, smiling and striding across the floor to hug her daughter. "You look exhausted."

"I was up late packing." Marigold made herself return her mother's smile, and her sister's, and those of the friends in the room, as though she didn't have a care in the world. "I'm home for good."

"Eeee!" Rose squealed. She bounded off the end of the bed and dashed forward.

"Careful." Marigold held the wooden box over her head. "I brought this to you." She looked past her sister's shoulder. "It's yours."

"The goldfinch!" Rose's gray-green eyes widened then began to sparkle with tears. "Oh, Mari, it should be yours, not mine."

Marigold's lips felt stiff. "You're the first one to marry, and this was created for the lady Colin Grassick loved. So it's yours."

"But you'll get married." Rose exchanged a glance with Momma.

"Someday," one of Rose's friends murmured.

"God knows my future." Marigold's face felt hot.

"Take it, Rose." Marigold held out the box.

"But—"

"Take it," the Marsh sisters overrode Rose's protest.

Rose took the box, her face pink with pleasure, her eyes bright with tears but dancing. "I never thought I'd marry, let alone first."

"So," Marigold said with too much briskness, "what can I do to help?"

Nothing, apparently. Momma, Rose, friends, and cousins had taken charge of all the wedding preparations from finding housing for the guests coming from long distances, to cooking, to decorating the church for the ceremony or the yard for the reception. Marigold did have to have her bridesmaid dress, purchased in the event she could participate, altered because she'd lost weight sometime in the past year.

It was a bright blue silk confection that brought out the green of her eyes when she took off the hat that matched. But she wouldn't. This was Rose's day to shine.

And shine she did. No stunning white gown sewn with seed pearls and handmade lace compared to the glow of joy radiating from every fiber of Rose's being. Her face, her eyes, even her hair shimmered with a sparkle that brought tears of joy to Marigold's eyes. She was so happy for her sister.

She wanted that joy for herself.

Pleasure in Rose's happiness held Marigold up throughout

the day in which she had nothing to do but watch others work. After fifteen months of rarely sitting down except to read to the children or mend, idleness made her want to run up and down the steps for exercise. But she didn't want to disturb her carefully coiffed hair, the dress, or the masses of flowers. . . .

She'd wanted her bridesmaids to wear rich, rose pink. Roses bloomed in June.

And dreams died.

No, she mustn't feel sorry for herself. Tears would ruin her face and her dress and Rose's joy.

"It's time to go," Momma called from the foyer.

Carriages decorated with white satin ribbons stood waiting in front of the house to take them to the church. Momma, Father, and Rose climbed into the first one. Marigold joined the bridesmaids in the second one. Whips cracked. The horses tugged the vehicles forward and through the streets to the church, its bell announcing the happy occasion.

"Lucian's here," Priscilla pointed out.

Marigold tried not to look or ask.

"He's with Carrie Grassick," Priscilla added. "Look." She pointed out the window.

Carrie, like all the Grassicks, was lovely, with her smooth black hair and brilliant green eyes, fair skin, and a willowy figure. Like everyone else still outside the church, she and Lucian turned toward the carriages. Her left hand rested on Lucian's arm.

Even from twenty feet away, Marigold couldn't miss the sunlight sparkling off the diamond ring displayed outside Carrie's glove.

eleven

The knock sounded on the front door too early for a social call. Gordon rose from behind the desk now void of ledgers, of business correspondences, or invitations. Only a map of Alaska spread out before him so he could dream over its mountains and uninhabited spaces. He should answer the door. Mrs. Cromwell was busy helping the girls dress for the day and the new nurserymaid applicant was due to arrive at eleven o'clock.

"And if she's arrived at eight o'clock instead," Gordon grumbled, "I'll send her packing. I won't have a female around who can't listen to instructions."

Jaw set, he yanked open the door.

"Good morning," Marigold said with too bright a smile to be anything but forced and brittle.

"What are you doing here?" he demanded.

"You advertised for a nurserymaid. I thought I'd apply for the position." The smile cracked, and her lower lip quivered. "I don't have anything else to do."

"I'm fairly certain that the position's been filled."

And his heart shouldn't be leaping about like a fish joyous to find a multitude of flies skimming over the surface of its pond, without a one being attached to a hook.

Or was it?

Gordon looked at Marigold's face, the eyes shadowed, the skin pale, her hair in disarray. In the morning sunshine, she glowed like a precious statue, beautiful and rare.

And the hook drove deep, its barbed end driving deep into his heart.

"Come in," he said.

Go away! his heart shouted. *For your own sake, go!*

He stepped back and allowed her to enter. She carried only a small valise.

"Your luggage?" he asked. "Or is this a brief visit?"

"I never even unpacked and brought a few more things." She set down the valise as though it weighed more than she did. "It's at the station. I walked here."

"After you must have traveled all night." Gordon clasped his hands behind his back to stop himself from reaching out and embracing her. He shouldn't be happy to see her. He'd told her to go. He'd told her to resume her normal life, so he could resume his without her standing about, judging him on his actions.

Yet there she stood, fatigued, a little grubby, smelling of coal smoke from the train and the coffee staining the front of her ugly gray gown.

Marigolds should never be gray. They should never droop with tiredness. Their eyes shouldn't convey sorrow, nor their lips curve any way but upward.

His fingers twitched with the urge to tug a corner of her mouth upward until she smiled again. Or if he kissed her. . .

He curled his hands in on themselves to make them behave. She was a maidservant in his home.

No, she wasn't. She was a young lady with no business standing in his foyer. And he had no business being so happy to see her, to feel like a prayer he hadn't uttered had been answered.

"I've made arrangements to borrow the Morrises' coachman when necessary, so I will send him for your trunk."

"Then I may stay?" Her face lit with that smile he so wanted to see. Her curls bounced. "Thank you. It's only been three days, but. . .Mr. Chambers, I didn't have anywhere else to go."

"Your family didn't want you?" He let all his incredulity at that ring through.

"No, I mean, yes. That is—"

"Miss Marigold!" Ruby's cry rang loudly enough to be

heard all the way to the beach. Her footfalls thundered down the steps.

Gordon stepped out of the way just in time to avoid being bowled over as his niece charged for Marigold, arms outstretched. Marigold dropped to her knees in time to catch the child in full flight.

"You came back." Ruby wrapped her arms around Marigold's neck. "I told Beryl you would. She said you wouldn't 'cause you were going to a wedding and would get engaged again, but I said you'd come back 'cause you promised never to leave us alone."

"She didn't leave us alone." With more dignity, but considerable speed, Beryl descended the steps. "Uncle Gordon is here."

"Yes, but he doesn't have time for us and doesn't help me with my arithmetic or piano." Ruby shot Gordon a glare that stung. "He wants us to go away to school."

"A school will have more girls your age and better teachers than I am." Marigold released Ruby to hug Beryl. "Don't you want that?"

"I have to stay here for Mommy and Daddy." Ruby stuck her fingers in her mouth.

Beryl sighed and pulled them out again. "You'll be here until you die, too."

Marigold laughed. "I've missed you." She cast Gordon a sidelong glance. "All of you. It makes me happier than I've been since I left."

"The wedding?" He began to inquire.

"Have you girls gone for a walk yet?" Marigold broke in. "I hope not. I missed the sea."

"We haven't done anything since you left," Beryl announced. "Uncle Gordon is too busy trying to get rid of us, and Mrs. Cromwell is too busy interviewing people for your position."

"Oh, of course she is." Dismay tightened Marigold's face. She glanced at Gordon. "I'm intruding, aren't I? You've likely found someone."

Gordon opened his mouth to repeat that he was fairly certain he would offer the job to the woman coming in three hours, but the words wouldn't come. "I have an interview or two with candidates Mrs. Cromwell finds acceptable."

"What's acceptable?" Ruby asked.

"Good enough." Marigold tugged on one of the child's braids. "Like your hair isn't. It looks as bad as mine."

"She doesn't have a stain on her dress," Beryl pointed out. "You do."

"Oh, dear." Marigold flushed nearly as red as her hair. "Should I go change?"

"You look like you should rest." Gordon wanted her out of his vicinity before he hugged her like the girls and told her how much he'd missed her, too. The house no longer echoed as though empty of even the children. It rang with Marigold's sparkling voice, vibrated with her energy. "I'm leaving for the boathouse."

"You found something?" Marigold gave him her full attention.

"No, I have a potential buyer and need to inspect the boats before I can think of selling."

"You're going to sell the boats?" Beryl asked.

"As soon as I can."

"Can we go out on them before you do?" Beryl persisted.

"No." Ruby backed to the steps, her fingers in her mouth. "No, no, no. I won't. I can't—"

"Ruby." Gordon and Marigold reached the child at the same time.

Gordon crouched before her and took her hands in his. "Sweetheart, the boats won't hurt you."

"They hurt Mommy and Daddy. They went away because of the boat."

"No, Ruby." Gordon caught a tear on her cheek with the knuckle of one hand. "The storm made the boat go down. It was a squall that took them by surprise."

"Mr. Tripp told them not to go out," Beryl announced.

Gordon swung around to face her, nearly losing his balance. "What do you mean? I thought he'd been dismissed."

"He got dismissed a few weeks later," Marigold said.

Gordon's stomach twisted. "I'm not sure I like the sound of this."

"The ledgers—"

"Not in front of the children." Gordon cut off Marigold's question.

Beryl scowled at him. "People never say interesting things in front of us. You'd think we're babies."

"We don't want to say anything bad if it isn't true." Gordon tried to smile at her. "Let's talk about taking that boat ride soon. Right now I have business to conduct, and Miss Marigold needs a nap. Where's Mrs. Cromwell?"

"She's in the kitchen," Beryl answered.

"She said she needs a cup of tea after getting us ready." Ruby giggled. "She wants me to dress just like Beryl, but she has new shoes and I don't."

"And your hair won't stay braided." Beryl tossed her head. "Mine never comes undone."

"Pride goeth before a fall, Beryl," Marigold said, then grimaced and raised a hand to her eyes. "I do believe I will take that nap."

"Did you leave right after the wedding?" Gordon couldn't stop himself from asking.

She nodded. "I left as soon as my sister and her new husband departed for their wedding journey. I couldn't. . . stay." She yawned, perhaps the reason for the hitch in her voice, but Gordon didn't think so.

With all his heart, he wanted to know what was wrong, why she looked so sad, why she had come back when he'd said he didn't want her there, why home had become so onerous to her. He opened his mouth to ask her to take some refreshment in the library before she went to her room, a room still ready for her, but snapped his lips together without speaking.

Concern for others led to trouble. He was better off alone and praying for them.

"I'll be on my way," he said and swung toward the door. "I must be back by eleven."

"When is the boat trip?" Beryl asked.

"There's room for us on a boat tomorrow." He tossed the answer over his shoulder. "We'll go tomorrow."

"No." Ruby's protest was the last thing he heard as the front door clicked shut behind him.

He wished his heart would click shut with so little effort. For ten years, he'd managed to keep the door on caring too much for others firmly closed, usually locked. If he saw others in trouble, he prayed for them and moved on. He did not get involved. Doing so had cost him too much in the past. Yet his niece's fear of going on the water disturbed him. Marigold's reappearance and obvious unhappiness tore at him.

"God, I need to get away sooner than later."

A passerby on the sidewalk gave him an odd look. Gordon smiled. He must remember that he was in the middle of a town, a small town bursting at the seams with summer visitors. Praying out loud wasn't an option for him.

Nor was a peaceful walk. He passed too many people. Most of them knew him by now, or knew who he was. He passed the eyesore of the derelict elephant and wished he could still climb to the top. Even with others there, he had felt alone when he gazed out to sea, imagined sailing over the horizon.

He'd sailed over that horizon and back again. He'd climbed over the mountains and back again. Alaska was the closest thing to a frontier left for him to discover. It was the last place where he had a chance to build his own fortune, to prove to his father that he would amount to something.

He'd done a poor job of it so far. Every penny he'd earned had gone into his next excursion. The sale of the boating business would go into his next excursion. This time, he wouldn't fail. He would be properly equipped. He'd planned.

And his brother's death had interrupted those plans.

Marigold threatened to interrupt those plans.

He stopped in the middle of the boardwalk and stared out to sea, wondering where such a notion had come from. Marigold might help him make his escape. He could trust her. If she truly had nowhere else to go, she could stay at the house once he left. He could hire a companion for her, to make things respectable. They could keep the house for the girls, the girls would have a place to return for holidays, and someone who loved them with whom they could stay.

Excited with his idea, Gordon hastened his steps to the boathouse, secured a place for them on the boat for the following day, and headed home to talk to Marigold about her future.

About her present. As much as he told himself he needed to know because what had happened at home impacted her ability to continue working for him, he admitted to himself that he wanted to know because some of her sunshine had clouded.

His wanting to know was good reason for him to be gone as soon as possible.

Piano scales and the aroma of baking gingerbread greeted him when he entered the house. Moments later, the applicant arrived, fresh-faced, cheerful, and far too young.

"I'm sorry," he told her, "I need someone more. . .matronly."

The young woman glanced at Mrs. Cromwell, who had joined him for the interview. She shook her head. Neither female knew what Gordon wanted in a woman he hired. He didn't either, not until he talked to Marigold.

Once the girl left, he followed his ears to the sound of the piano and found Marigold presiding over Ruby's practice.

"Miss McCorkle?" he asked.

She glanced up.

Ruby slid off the stool and raced across the room. "I can do two octaves without making a mistake. Do you want to hear?"

"Of course I do." He couldn't say anything else.

Ruby demonstrated her growing skill. Then Beryl showed him how she had improved, playing a simple piece.

"Now you play, Miss Marigold," the girls urged.

Gordon didn't encourage it. Nor did he discourage it. Marigold's playing was worth listening to. By the time she finished the sonata, Mrs. Cromwell entered with milk for the girls and coffee for the adults, gingerbread and cookies for everyone.

So the day went. Every time he tried to talk to Marigold, she vanished behind the girls' needs to eat, to practice, to go play with the cat in the yard. Not until after supper, when the girls settled down to read or draw on their own in the parlor, did he track her down in the kitchen, where she was washing dishes.

"Why did you come back?" he asked without the preamble of social niceties.

She rinsed a plate before setting it in the rack to dry and turning to face him. "My father doesn't need me working in the business. He's an exporter, you see, which is how I met my fiancé—my former fiancé. I'm afraid he thinks I'll fall for someone else, who–who's unsuitable. I find my mother's charity work tedious, and—and—" She snapped her teeth together and returned to the washing up.

"And?" Gordon prompted.

"I'm back. That's what matters. If you don't want me to stay, I won't, of course, but those little girls need someone who loves them, and I love them."

"I know you do."

And he loved her. He loved her so much he knew he should send her away before he hurt her, before she buried herself in Cape May and never found someone who wanted to love her.

He didn't want to love her, didn't want to face the pain and grief of being pushed aside for someone with better prospects, for a man worthy of her generous heart and loving spirit.

"You can stay." Huskiness invaded his voice. "Tomorrow we'll take the girls out on one of the excursion boats."

"Ruby's scared." Marigold glanced at him, her eyes clouded.

"I know. It's the best way to get her over her fear. And she must. She can't go through life being afraid of boats."

"Unless she wants to move to Kansas or something." Marigold smiled.

"Even so. . . If she's too frightened, we'll come back."

"It's because of her parents, you know." Marigold began to wash dishes again, her hands nearly elbow-deep in sudsy water. "She can't accept that they won't come back. I don't know how to fix that for her."

"Time, I think. But perhaps going on the water will help her understand. . .something." Not wanting to leave, despite his business with Marigold concluded, Gordon picked up a dish towel and began to dry the stacked plates. "So tell me about the wedding."

"Rose was beautiful. My mother had everything planned to perfection. Everyone asked me why I—" She ducked her head. Curls cascaded across her cheek.

"Why you gave up your marriage plans for near strangers?"

"I wasn't the one who gave them up."

"If he wouldn't wait for you, then he doesn't deserve you."

"That's what my sister said. But when he arrived at the wedding with—I told them I was committed to the girls here. And Lucian—" She heaved a sigh. "I didn't want to stay any longer than I had to. I missed everyone here so much, and the river isn't nearly as nice as the ocean."

"Would you like to stay on even after I leave?" Gordon asked.

She jumped, sending a glass plopping into the water with a spray of suds that soaked the front of her gown.

He smiled. "I didn't mean to startle you. I'm only thinking about this, but if you really have nowhere to go, I can hire a companion for you, if you'll stay on and manage the house. It will give the girls somewhere to go on school holidays."

"They'd rather come home to you, Mr. Chambers. They need their family."

"Odd you would say that when you have chosen to leave yours."

"Yes, well, staying where everyone knows me was too—" She sighed. "I'll go back if you choose to stay here."

"I can't stay." He stacked several plates before he admitted, "This isn't my house. It's my father's. He tossed me out of it and wouldn't welcome me back if he were still alive. I'll return to stay when I can buy a house of my own."

"Hmm." She collected a pan from the top of the stove and dunked it into the dishwater. "I can't imagine any father tossing his son out of his house forever. Nothing is that bad."

"I ruined someone else's life, hurt the family's reputation. . . . He was justified in his actions. Even Gerald sided with him." He lifted the stack of plates and carried them to their cupboard before he said too much, before she asked him to say more.

She didn't ask him anything. When he returned with a dry dish towel, she tilted her head to one side and smiled up at him. "I'll tell you about my father sending me packing, if you'll share your story."

twelve

Marigold didn't know what possessed her to make such a personal suggestion to her employer. Yet he didn't feel like her employer, standing there with a dish towel over his arm and his shirt cuffs wet. He looked like something she had never envisioned Lucian being—a spouse who was a companion, not just a vague figure across the breakfast table.

The revelation struck her like a rolling pin between the shoulder blades, and she blurted out, "I never loved him."

Gordon dropped the glass he was drying. He dove for the shining fragments. Marigold dove for the pieces. Their heads collided.

"Oof." Marigold jerked back, slipped in a patch of water, and landed on her seat.

"I am so sorry." That treacherous corner of his mouth twitching, Gordon leaned down and offered his hands. "Are you all right?"

"I think so." She tried to get her feet under her. Her heels tangled in her skirts, and she moved no further than her knees.

"Here." Gordon clasped her by the waist and lifted her to her feet—and didn't let go.

She knew she should tell him she was all right, that he could release her without worrying she would fall again. She wanted to tell him she would go to her room now and not bring up anything personal.

She looked into his deep brown eyes, saw the sparkle even in the murky gaslight of the kitchen, and lowered her lashes, ready, willing, perhaps too eager, and not caring in that moment when his lips met hers.

The contact lasted no more than a heartbeat. It was the best moment in the past year and a half of Marigold's life. She wanted to run off to her room, write the moment down, savor every detail of his tender expression, his scent of sunshine and lemons, his lips as gentle as a summer breeze, though they flooded her with a hurricane gale of longing.

"I. . .suppose that was completely inappropriate." His voice emerged as though he spoke from a dry throat. "You work for me."

"I can leave your employment."

"You just lost your fiancé."

"He never should have been my fiancé." She spoke in a breathless rush, trying to get everything out before he walked away. "He wasn't in love with me, or he'd have waited for me, instead of getting himself engaged to one of the Grassick girls. And I couldn't have loved him, or I wouldn't—"

No, she wouldn't humiliate herself by admitting she loved him until he told her he felt more than an attraction for her. One humiliation at the hands of a male was quite enough for one summer.

"Have just let you kiss me," she concluded.

"Perhaps not." His smile was gentle, his fingers against her cheek gentler. "Now I understand why you came back. Facing that kind of humiliation must have been difficult for a proud lady like you. But I can't let you hurt yourself by entangling yourself in my life. Kissing you was. . .wonderful. Believe me. I'd do it again in a moment if I thought it would benefit either of us. But it won't, Marigold. It was an error in judgment, and I'm too good at making errors in judgment to be responsible for anyone other than myself."

"No, no, I don't believe that. You knew you had to stay here longer than you thought."

"But stayed away too long."

"You—"

"Hush." He pressed his finger to her lips. "I won't let you make an error in judgment, either. And saying things to me right now will likely be just that."

She wanted to argue with him further but feared he was

right, if that concerned how she felt about him.

Or maybe just thought she felt about him.

Yet because she cared, however deeply that caring ran, she couldn't bear the pain flickering in his eyes, the pain of his words, claiming he made poor judgments. She wanted, needed, to say something to ease that burden.

She took a deep breath. "Perhaps you depend on yourself instead of the Lord for your decisions, and that's why you think they go awry."

"My relationship with the Lord is my concern." His face tightened. "Go to your room, Miss McCorkle. I'll finish clearing up in here."

"But—"

"Go, or I'll consider the worst of my choices has been to allow you to stay a minute after I got here." He smiled without humor. "Which it probably was."

"Gor—" With an effort, Marigold closed her mouth, turned on her heel, and raced up to her room.

For solace, she pushed aside the latter part of their encounter and concentrated on those moments of closeness. He'd kissed her.

Lucian had kissed her, too. They'd been engaged. She'd liked it.

When Gordon kissed her, she'd loved it. Because she loved him? She thought she did. She figured she had for most of the nearly four weeks she'd known him, if that was possible. At least for the past few days. At least since he'd opened the door to her and welcomed her back with a look she could only describe as joyous.

Because he loved her, too?

How she wanted to think so, but dared not. She must keep herself aloof, protect her pride, protect her soul. She would become the perfect maidservant, beginning with having the girls ready for the boating excursion the following morning.

❧

But the next morning, Ruby was missing. Marigold slipped

into the girls' room to wake them up and found no child in the second bed.

"When did Ruby get up?" Marigold demanded of Beryl.

"Dunno." Beryl yawned and rubbed her eyes. "Sleeping."

"Perhaps she went downstairs." Marigold rushed down to the kitchen. "Is Ruby here?"

Mrs. Cromwell turned from the stove. "I haven't seen her this morning. Maybe she's with Mr. Gordon."

"Where's he?"

"In his library."

Marigold darted through the door separating the kitchen from the rest of the house and charged into the library. "Where's Ruby?"

Gordon dropped his coffee cup, spilling brown liquid across his desk and a map.

"I'm so sorry." Marigold made the apology in a breathless rush. "Ruby isn't in her bed, and Mrs. Cromwell hasn't seen her."

Before she finished speaking, Gordon was on his feet and reaching for the coat hanging on the back of his chair. "Finish searching the house. I'll look outside. If she's not there, I'll go to the Morrises' and get help."

Ruby wasn't inside. Beryl, Mrs. Cromwell, and Marigold searched from the attic to the cellar and found no sign of the little girl.

"She never goes anywhere alone." Trying not to cry, Marigold stood on the front porch and insisted her brain work on a solution. "She knows better."

"It's my fault," Beryl said and burst into tears.

"What do you mean?" Marigold put her arms around the child. "How can this be your fault?"

Beryl shook her head, sobbing. "I called her a baby for being afraid to go on the boat. I said—I said if—if we were nicer children Uncle Gordon wouldn't go away. And. . .I'm so sorry."

"Why did you say those things to her, Beryl?" Marigold sat back on her haunches and looked into the girl's face. "Why were you so mean to her?"

"Because—because. . ." Beryl looked away. "She never liked the boats and keeps me from going on them."

"I see." At least Marigold thought she understood. "Well, Beryl, now none of us can go because Ruby isn't here."

Beryl bowed her head and scuffed at the floorboards with the toe of her shoe. "She's probably in the elephant."

"You know? You've known all along?" Marigold shot to her feet, her hands crushing fistfuls of her skirt. "Why didn't you tell us? Never mind that now. We'll talk about it later. Go to your room and stay there."

"You're angry with me." Beryl recommenced crying.

"Yes, Beryl, I am. But right now, finding your sister is more important."

"But she's the one who's naughty."

"You're both naughty." Marigold spun on her heel and raced for the sidewalk.

The elephant, old and rickety, must be dangerous. Signs told people to stay away. It smelled of rotting lumber and rusting metal. Rats probably lived inside the enormous legs, and if Ruby tried to climb the steps, she was likely to fall through a disintegrating board and break something vital.

Marigold ran. She held her skirts as high as the tops of her shoes to keep herself from tripping on them. She passed people she knew and gawking strangers, ice cream sellers and barking dogs. She ran toward the blot on the Cape May landscape and ignored shouts for her to stop, calls of her name, warnings to slow down.

She started calling Ruby's name the minute the elephant heaved into view. And she kept running toward the beast, past signs that warned people away, past the signs that had once advertised on the monstrous sides. She hollered for Ruby until her throat hurt.

At the door to one of the elephant's legs, she stopped. Her heart raced. Her breath rasped in her throat.

The door stood open.

She laid her hand on the frame.

"You can't go in there, miss." A brawny workman shoved between Marigold and the door. "It's dangerous."

"I know." She bent double against a stitch in her side. "Little girl. . . Lost. . . Think—inside. . ."

The man murmured something that sounded like a prayer. A prayer!

Marigold leaned against the elephant's scarred side and closed her eyes. She hadn't stopped to pray. She'd determined to find Ruby on her own.

"Please, God, help me find her," she whispered into her hands. "I need to—"

"I'll go look, miss." The workman pushed the door open further. "What's her name?"

"Ruby. She's only six."

"Too young to be on her own." He gave Marigold a censorious glance.

She frowned at him. "I didn't let her be on her own. She slipped out of the house without us knowing."

"Huh." Mouth set as though he were eating limes, the workman tramped into the elephant.

His footfalls rang hollowly. His voice sounded as though he called into a bucket. The silence in response sounded even louder.

"Ruby." Marigold stepped to the doorway of the elephant. The stench of mildew and rot assailed her nostrils. "I'm here. Don't be frightened."

She wanted to promise the child that she wouldn't have to go out on a boat. But Marigold couldn't make that kind of promise. It was up to Gordon, and he believed she should go out on the water to get over her fear. He said that way worked the best. He'd said it as though he knew what he was talking about.

She couldn't imagine Gordon Chambers afraid of anything. He was too big, too strong, too sure of what he wanted. Or didn't want—her.

"Ruby," the workman called.

"Please, Ruby, answer if you're here," Marigold reiterated.

No small voice responded. The workman's boots tramped back down the steps. The gunshot crack of a splintering tread ricocheted off the walls. The workman muttered something and leaped to the bottom of the steps.

"She's not here, miss," he told Marigold.

She resisted the urge to wipe a cobweb from his hat brim and crossed her arms over her chest. "You're sure? You looked everywhere? What about the other legs, the trunk, the top?"

"She's not here." The workman moved forward, compelling Marigold to step back. "I didn't see any footprints in the dirt."

"I see. Well then, thank you for looking." Marigold turned away and plowed through the small crowd staring toward the elephant. Her heart ached. She pounded one fist into the other. "God, why do I keep failing? Why do I keep losing? Why do I—"

She heard herself, heard one word repeated again and again: I. . .I. . .I. . .

She stumbled to a halt on the pavement and leaned against a lamppost, her knees too weak to support her, her pride enough to keep her from sinking to the ground in front of all the holidaymakers. She tried to think. Her head whirled. Sun and sound intensified until the brightness and volume of shouting youths, shrieking children, and chattering adults would explode like dynamite inside her head.

"Marigold—that is, Miss McCorkle?" Gordon Chambers touched her arm. "Are you all right?"

"No. Yes. I—"

There was that word again, selfish, self-centered, prideful. *God, how far do I need to fall?*

She raised her gaze to Gordon's face, her vision blurred. "We have to find Ruby. Beryl said she'd be in the elephant, but she's not there."

"You didn't go in, did you?" Gordon looked alarmed.

Marigold shook her head.

"Good. It can't be safe. But how do you know she's not there?"

"A workman came around and looked for me." Marigold wiped her eyes on her sleeve. "But now where do we go?"

"Where else does she like to be?" Gordon asked.

"The lighthouse?"

They turned toward the towering structure at the point of the cape, where it guided ships to a safe passage into Delaware Bay.

"I don't like it, but there are always so many visitors there she would be safe." Gordon rubbed his temples as though his head hurt. "Shall we go look?"

"Yes, please." Without thinking, Marigold tucked her hand into the crook of his arm, as they headed for the lighthouse at a trot. "We have gone there twice. She likes looking out to sea to find dolphins."

"I used to do that as a youth, too. I missed the dolphins once I left here. Of course I saw them on my travels, but somehow seeing them from the lighthouse was more enjoyable. Maybe because I saw them from so far away no one on land could see them yet. It was like being first."

"You love it here, don't you?" Marigold spoke so softly, she doubted he heard her over the boisterous visitors surrounding them. He said nothing for several blocks, then without warning, he covered her hand with his and inclined his head.

"Then why leave?" She spoke in a low voice, afraid to speak louder for fear of breaking the contact between them.

Which meant she should break it. She should not be loving the sensation of Gordon Chambers, her employer, cradling her fingers between his large palm and muscled forearm. Not wishing he would kiss her again.

Once more, he remained silent and without expression for so long she thought he hadn't heard her. Then he gestured toward the boathouse, where visitors lined up to board the excursion boats. "It has to do with a boat. And me being young and impulsive and stupid and wanting my own way—like too many youths with more money than sense and discipline." He grimaced. "I had free rein of the boats that weren't being used at the time. Gerald and I always understood that I'd get the boathouse, and he'd get the real estate business. My father was clear that's how he'd divide up the inheritance. And it would have been all right if—"

"Mr. Chambers?" The voice rang over roar of surf and shouts of merrymakers on the beach.

Marigold and Gordon stopped, turned to the shouting man.

Dennis Tripp charged up to them, then stood gasping for air, his hands on the threadbare thighs of his trousers.

"What is it?" Gordon demanded. "Speak now. We don't have time. My niece is missing."

"I know where she is." Tripp straightened. "I was looking for coins on the beach—" His face flushed at this admission of his poverty. "I saw her on one of the boats. I thought she must be with you, but you're here."

"She couldn't have," Gordon declared.

"She wouldn't have," Marigold said at the same time.

Tripp looked frustrated. "Why would I lie to you?"

"You lied to me about the ledgers," Gordon pointed out. "You claimed Randall was cheating me, but neither Miss McCorkle nor I found anything wrong with them."

"Look again." Tripp's face tightened as though he were about to cry. "They're in code or something. I know the boats are in ill repair. But after you get your niece back."

"And how do I do that?" Gordon sounded belligerent.

Marigold understood why—worry and frustration. Not a single boat remained at the jetty.

"Find a way. That entire operation should be shut down until the boats are inspected." Tripp turned away. "But you don't have to believe me. I just pray no one gets hurt, someone like your niece, until you do."

He stalked off and vanished into the crowd.

Marigold looked up at Gordon. "We must find someone

with a boat to help us find her. Someone else will lend us a craft, I'm sure."

"I am, too, but we have no idea which way to look or for which craft." A muscle in his jaw bunched. "The man couldn't bother to tell us."

"Or we were rude to him and sent him away before we asked."

"He should have—" Gordon sighed. "You're right. Let's find him and ask. He can't have gone far."

But he had gone somewhere. They searched for ten minutes without spotting a little man with ragged clothes and a sad yet peaceful expression.

"He's just a troublemaker," Gordon grumbled. "Now we've wasted time when we should have been hunting for Ruby."

Movement on the water caught Marigold's attention. "One of the boats is coming back in."

Without another word, they raced for the jetty and the docking excursion boat. Laughing, chattering families poured over the gangway and onto dry land. From snatches of conversation, they'd seen only one dolphin, but it was amazing to people who didn't live near the sea.

The instant the last passenger disembarked, Gordon, with Marigold behind, leaped aboard the boat and grabbed one of the crewmen. "I'm looking for my niece. She's a little girl—"

"You're going to have to get a ticket to get aboard, sir." The crewman was polite but firm. "I don't give out information—"

Gordon grasped the man's shoulder. "My niece is only six and may have sneaked aboard."

"No little girls, sir. Now, if you don't get off this boat, I'll have to call the police—"

"I own this boat." Gordon shook the man.

"Get your hands off of me." The crewman punched Gordon in the middle. "I know the owner, and it's not you."

Gordon barely flinched from the blow, but he removed his hand from the man's shoulder, though curled it into a fist. "If you want to keep your position," he said in a deadly quiet voice, "you will answer my question. I don't know who you think owns this company, but I am Gordon Chambers, and the court will inform you that I own it by inheritance."

"I—I'm sorry." The man backed up, his hands in front of him. "I thought—we all thought—I'll get the skipper." He spun on his heel and charged aft.

Marigold touched Gordon's arm. "Are you all right?"

"Physically, yes. Otherwise—" He faced her abruptly. "Who does he think owns this company?"

"I don't know." Marigold felt sick, not from the gentle rise and fall of the deck as the tide sloshed against the pier, but from the apprehension that Dennis Tripp was right and something was terribly wrong besides Ruby going missing, and not taking him seriously enough was the worst judgment either she or Gordon had made.

thirteen

Gordon grasped Marigold's arm. "Stop anyone else from coming aboard. I'll find the skipper myself."

"What are we going to do?" She looked pale, frightened.

"Find Ruby, if she is aboard one of these boats."

"I think she is. I think Mr. Tripp's right."

"I agree. That crewman should have known who owns this company. That tells me something is not right here." He released Marigold. "Let's hope Tripp's not right about the poor repairs."

Gordon should have taken an active role in the business instead of planning to leave as soon as possible. He should have been more responsible toward others, toward his nieces.

Yet once again, he wasn't thinking and was taking actions that hurt those he cared about, like seeking a school for the girls, like kissing Marigold.

He'd thought going through the ledgers would be enough, but of course it wasn't. He should have known that as soon as Marigold pointed out the name discrepancies. But he couldn't be bothered with details because they got in the way of his plans to sell the business as soon as the court had probated Gerald's will and gave him the go-ahead.

"God, please let Ruby and the boat be all right. Or let her be on land somewhere safe."

He reached the pilothouse, where the skipper of the craft and crewmen stood at the wheel, talking in low voices. They turned on Gordon, their faces tight.

"I'm Gordon Chambers, the owner of this boating business," Gordon said. "We are going to go on your usual route and find the other boats in the event my niece is aboard one of them."

"I can't do that without Mr. Randall's permission, sir." The skipper spoke with more respect than the crewman had, but his bearded jaw was set in a pugnacious line.

"Mr. Randall isn't aboard. I am." Gordon glanced through the window and saw Marigold disappear into the cabin.

Seeking Ruby? Of course she would, bless her.

"Mr. Randall won't object, Captain," Gordon said with as much pleasantry as he could conjure. "Even if he does, I am in a position to ensure nothing happens to your position."

"But I don't know you." The skipper glanced toward shore.

Several people, who looked like passengers, lined up at the foot of the gangway. Lawrence Randall was pushing through them.

Gordon stepped in front of the skipper again. "You don't recognize my resemblance to my brother?"

"Why should I?"

"Because he owned—"

"We'll ask Mr. Randall now," the crewman said and shoved past Gordon.

He followed, along with the skipper. Marigold was nowhere around.

"Sir," the skipper called to Randall, "this man insists I take the boat out to look for his niece."

"Then, by all means, do it." Randall smiled ingratiatingly. "Of course, we'll disappoint a number of people, which won't do the business any good, but it's his company to ruin, if he doesn't want to sell it for much."

A bell louder than any ship's timer boomed in Gordon's head. He frowned at the company manager. "Would you like to buy it, Mr. Randall?"

"Beyond my price." Waving, Randall headed down the gangway and began speaking to the waiting passengers.

"What are you waiting for?" Gordon asked the skipper. "Take this boat on the tour the rest take. We'll try to intercept them and see if my niece is aboard."

"If she ain't aboard this one," the crewman grumbled.

"People who can't take care of their families. . ."

Apparently thinking better of whatever he'd been about to say, he turned away and followed the skipper back to the pilothouse.

Gordon began to hunt around chairs and tables set out on deck. They all looked well, painted with bright, white paint and clean. The deck, too, seemed to have been painted recently. Brass on railings and the cabin door gleamed in the sunlight.

Surely Tripp was wrong.

Gordon opened the door to the cabin. It resembled a luxurious parlor, with velvet-covered sofas and chairs set in groupings around the chamber. The windows could have been cleaner, and he caught one or two worn places on the cushions; however, keeping windows clean on a vessel and repairing furniture used as much as this was, was nearly impossible.

Calmed by the outwardly good appearance of the craft, as well as the familiar *chug-chug-chug* of the engine, Gordon headed out the forward end of the cabin in search of Ruby, in search of Marigold.

He heard her scream a moment after the boat left the wharf.

"Marigold?" His heart raced faster than the screw pushing the boat forward. "Marigold, where are you?"

"Here." Her voice was faint, muffled. "I'm. . .fine."

The hitch in her voice told him she wasn't quite telling the truth.

He followed the sound until he saw a companionway leading below. Nothing should be down there but a small cabin, perhaps, for the crew, the engine room, and a hold full of fuel.

And Marigold. She sat on the next to the bottom step, her foot caught in a hole in the bottom tread.

"I'm a bit clumsy, as you know." She smiled up at him, but the whiteness of her face betrayed pain.

"My dear girl." Gordon moved past her with care, testing

each step to ensure it could hold his weight. "How did this happen?"

"I was just coming down here, and all looked well. . . ."

It did. Like on the deck, the paint appeared fresh. But the board beneath was rotten.

The icy waters of the North Atlantic seemed to flow through Gordon's veins. Sick to his stomach, he knelt at Marigold's feet and worked her foot from the hole. Thanks to the high top of her shoe, she hadn't cut it, but her gasp of pain and his probing fingers told him the ankle was swelling.

"I think a sprain," he said. "I'll have to carry you up."

"You can't. And if Ruby's here. . ."

"I'll find her when I get you settled."

"I'm too heavy."

"No, you're not." Before she could argue further, Gordon scooped her into his arms and headed up the way he had come.

She remained stiff in his hold until they reached the top. Then she relaxed against him, her head lolling on his shoulder, one of her arms encircling his neck.

She wasn't a burden at all. He liked his arms around her. With her face so close to his, the yearning to kiss her nearly left him breathless.

His guilt stopped him. He had caused this, just like he had caused many of Louisa's troubles. He hadn't wanted anything to be wrong with the company—so selling it would be easy and quick—so he'd ignored the warnings.

"I'm so sorry, my dear." He brushed his lips across her brow. "So very sorry."

"I'm all right. I'm sure Ruby is all right. Now, put me down and go look for her."

"In here." He carried her into the cabin and set her on a sofa. "You may wish to remove your shoe in case your ankle swells more. Even if they are as ugly as your gray dresses, you don't want to ruin good shoes."

She laughed, brushed his hair off his forehead, and kissed his cheek. "Don't blame yourself for this."

"How can I not?" He turned and left as quickly as he could.

Hunting through every recess of the vessel, annoying two more crewmen down in the engine room, he sought for other signs of decay covered over with fresh paint. He found none. That didn't mean other problems didn't exist, problems he should have found.

"God, where did I go wrong?"

With no sign of Ruby aboard, he returned to the deck. He saw Marigold through the cabin window, wanted to go to her, but didn't dare. She deserved better than a man like this Lucian, who had jilted her because she'd asked him to wait, for a good reason, and she deserved better than a Gordon Chambers, who wanted things the way he wanted them—a life free of commitments, free of responsibility. . . .

"I'm despicable, Lord. I deserved to be rejected by my father."

Yet God was a father who hadn't rejected him for his shortcomings, for going his own way. Gordon paid lip service to being a Christian, yet how often had he asked God what he should do? Not when he tried to help Louisa and caused disaster. Not when he'd invested years of savings in a mine that had been paid out years earlier. Not when he'd returned to Cape May determined to leave as soon as possible so he could try to make another fortune and prove his father wrong to predict he'd come to no good.

He gripped the rail and gazed out across Delaware Bay. Vessels from the smallest of fishing boats to oceangoing liners scattered across the crystal blue waters. Smoke from engines drifted into the cloudless sky, and sometimes a burst of laughter mingled with the rumble of engines. It was a familiar scene, one that had told him he wanted to own this company when his father allowed it. Gerald had known it, had tried to keep their father from sending Gordon away permanently. And in the end, he'd done what he could to make things right.

"And I was going to destroy it by neglecting it and your children."

The scene blurred before Gordon's eyes. He was even hurting Gerald after his brother was gone from this earth.

"Lord, I can't go on like this. Please, show me what to do. Please—"

A shout rose from the bow. Gordon spun toward it and saw a crewman waving his arms and pointing. Ahead of them and to the starboard two or three points off the bow, a vessel similar to theirs wallowed in the glassy waters of the bay.

"She's sinking!" the man shouted. "We've gotta get alongside her."

This was God's answer—that his neglect, his desire to be away from Cape May, might cause the deaths of the fifty people aboard the other vessel?

"It can't be worse," he cried aloud.

But it could, for clinging to the rail between two elderly ladies, her pinafore already soaking wet, stood Ruby.

fourteen

"A rowboat. A dinghy." Gordon glanced around the deck as he shouted.

He saw neither craft.

"A line. Where's there a line?"

With a rope, he could possibly climb across, secure the line and. . .

No, if the other boat went down too quickly, they risked dragging this vessel down, too. He would have to swim, risk getting sucked under with the other boat, but possibly save Ruby and a few other people. He could throw chairs overboard for people to grab. Chairs would float.

He raced to the main deck and the furniture.

"Gordon." Marigold grasped his arm.

He turned. "I'm going overboard to help."

"No, you're not." Grimacing with pain, she held on to him with both hands. "It's too dangerous."

"I can't let Ruby drown, not like my brother. If I'd been here—"

"You couldn't have saved them."

"But I can save Ruby." He tried to pull free without hurting her, but her grip was fierce.

"Wait, Gordon. Look."

Across the gap of a hundred yards of water between his vessel and the one sinking in the bay, a dozen small boats had converged. Men, women, and a few youths swarmed around the foundering craft and aided the passengers in climbing over the railings and into safety.

"If I'd lost Ruby—" He stopped himself, his eyes widening. "Bring them here." He meant to shout the words. His voice emerged choked. His eyes blurred.

The boatmen seemed to understand anyway. They pulled toward his boat, where the crew gathered to receive wet, frightened, sobbing passengers onto the sun-drenched deck. Though her ankle had to pain her, Marigold worked alongside them. She must have hugged every lady and child lifted aboard.

Joining the efforts, Gordon wanted to hug her. Her dress was torn and sodden, her hair whipped around her face in a frizzy mass of fire, and her skin was beginning to turn pink from too much sun, but she was the most beautiful woman he had ever seen.

He reached her side just as Ruby came over the rail on the shoulders of a burly fisherman.

"Uncle Gordon." The child launched herself into his arms and clung. "I was naughty, and the boat was going to go down to the bottom. I almost made everyone drown like Mommy and Daddy."

"No, child, no." He held her close. "It wasn't your fault. It was mine. I've been a selfish, bitter fool."

Ruby stopped sobbing long enough to ask, "What's bitter?"

"Something nasty." He started to turn to Marigold again, but Dennis Tripp emerged from the crowd and stalked up to him.

"I told you. Those boats need work. Randall claims it was done, but he's a liar, and I won't mince words over it."

"Yes." Gordon met the man's gaze without flinching. "But the fault lies with me. I was too anxious to sell to look into matters carefully. If anyone was hurt, it's my fault."

"None of the boats should go out again until they're fully inspected," Tripp pronounced.

"They won't." Gordon glanced toward shore, knowing he said good-bye to his grubstake for a head start in Alaska. "I'm shutting the business down until we know all is well and safe. Can you—will you see to it, Mr. Tripp?"

"I'd be honored, sir." Tripp's face flushed as he ducked his head. "With the Lord's help, we'll set all to rights."

"Yes, with the Lord's help."

Past Tripp's shoulder, Gordon saw Marigold's face, her widened eyes, her mouth forming an *O*. He thought it was of approval. He hoped it was of approval as he added, "With the Lord's help and the help of those He has sent to be a part of my life."

In his arms, Ruby shivered but seemed to have stopped sobbing.

"We'll get you home as soon as we land," he told her.

Still carrying Ruby, he walked among the passengers, listening to their complaints, their praise, their anger. He blamed none of them for their outrage.

"You'll get your money back," he assured him. "I can't promise you more than that right now, as I'm closing the company until we're certain the boats are safe."

A few people protested that.

"Accidents happen, sir," one youth said. "And this was a great adventure."

"It could have been a great tragedy."

Ruby, sodden in his arms, was testimony to that.

As much as he wanted to rush straight home, he waited on deck with the skippers and crew from both boats while the passengers disembarked. When they were gone, he addressed his employees.

"Gentlemen, I want every excursion boat secured upon its return. A thorough inspection of each boat will be conducted, and proper repairs will be made before I will allow them to sail again. Passengers who've paid for canceled excursions will be refunded."

A murmur rose among the crewmen. They needed their jobs.

Ruby shivered in his arms. "I need to get my niece home, but I will return with further instructions. Dennis Tripp is in charge in my absence."

He nearly forgot about Marigold, until he heard a rustle behind him and turned to see her leaning against the rail, her face pinched with pain.

She smiled at him with tight lips. "Know anyone who can carry me?"

"I can. No one else here looks strong enough to carry you." He called to one of the dispersing crewmen. When the young man stopped and turned back, Gordon said, "I need your help with the young lady. Please carry my niece."

"I'm too big for you to carry," Marigold protested.

"No, you're not." Slowly, reluctantly, Gordon placed Ruby in the sailor's arms. The young man held her as though she were fragile, his face growing tender.

Ruby whimpered in objection.

"Miss Marigold hurt her ankle," Gordon told Ruby. "She can't walk."

"Your niece is safe with me, sir." The crewman stood motionless, while Gordon scooped Marigold into his arms.

"You can't walk six blocks with me." She tried to squirm free.

"You can't walk six feet; now be quiet." Gordon strode down the gangway, his precious burden slumped against his shoulder.

Burden. That's what he'd thought of his nieces and any idea of a wife—burdens to be avoided. He couldn't drop a burden he didn't carry. Yet, as he walked beside the young man carrying Ruby, Gordon experienced no fear that he would drop Marigold. She felt light, though she wasn't a small woman.

Could he possibly. . . ? Did he dare. . . ?

Beryl, Mrs. Cromwell, and Mrs. Morris sat on the front porch. The older women rose as the odd procession came around the corner.

Beryl leaped all five steps in a bound and raced to greet them. "You found her. Ruby, you are in trouble. Why are you wet? Why is Uncle Gordon carrying Miss Marigold?"

Ruby turned her face into the young man's shoulder and didn't answer.

"Did you go to the elephant like you said you would?" Beryl persisted.

"Later." Marigold leaned out of Gordon's hold and caught hold of Beryl's hand. "She's frightened and cold. I'll talk to her later. That is, your uncle will talk to her later." She glanced at him. "I don't have the authority to question Ruby. Not now, when I've failed her."

"How?" Gordon adjusted his hold on her so she couldn't slip away from him.

"I ignored the way Beryl talks to her. We sisters aren't always kind to each other. The things I said to Rose shame me."

"But they're in the past." Gordon smiled at her then turned to Mrs. Cromwell. "Will you be so kind as to run a hot bath for Ruby? I'm afraid Marigold can't climb the steps." To the crewman, he added, "Thank you for your help. You did admirable work today. I won't forget it."

"Please don't, sir. If you close the excursion company, we'll all be out of work. It's hard enough to find here in the winter."

Gordon sighed. "We'll see what condition things truly are in. But I'll do what I can for all of you."

The young man set Ruby on the porch, bade good-bye, and fairly raced down the street.

"Come along, Ruby, precious," Mrs. Cromwell said.

"Bring Marigold into the parlor," Mrs. Morris suggested. "We can have the doctor in to look at them both, and you can tell me what happened."

Gordon started up the steps. Seeing Beryl standing by the door, he said, "Go help Mrs. Cromwell with Ruby."

"I'm not a nurserymaid."

"Beryl," Gordon's voice cracked across the child's protest, "you are in enough trouble without talking back to me."

"I'm in trouble?" Beryl stared at him. "Why am I in trouble? I've stayed home all along like I'm supposed to."

Gordon glared at her. "You know what you did, so don't play innocent with me. We'll talk about your unkindness later. Now, go up to your room and help Mrs. Cromwell."

"Yes, sir." Head bowed, Beryl dragged her feet on her way into the house.

"Don't be mad at Beryl," Ruby said. "She doesn't mean to be mean."

"I did mean it." Beryl spun around at the foot of the steps, her face contorted with an effort not to shed the tears in her eyes. "I meant everything I said, but then you really were gone, and I was scared, and then I didn't mean all those things I said to you."

"You didn't?" Ruby reached out her arms to Beryl. "I love you, Beryl."

"I love you, too." Beryl ran back to the porch and hugged her younger sister. "We have to get along. We won't have anyone else once Uncle Gordon goes away."

"And he'll go away now, too, because I was bad." Ruby began to cry. "Just like Mommy and Daddy went away because I was naughty."

❧

Dressed alike in white frocks, Ruby and Beryl sat on the parlor sofa and wore similar expressions of apprehension and contrition. Marigold—attired in one of the gray gowns Gordon wanted to ask the laundry to burn next time they went out for cleaning—sat between the girls, one hand on either thin shoulder, her face set, as though she were angry or distressed.

Gordon's own insides squeezed and softened. Seeing them after the past hour he'd spent working out what to do with the business felt like the first cool, sweet drink of water after months of brackish ship's fare. He could drink in the sight of them for hours, days, years.

He shook his head to clear it of such nonsense. He didn't want or need any more time with them than necessary. The girls needed playmates their own age and a female who could teach them things girls needed to learn, and Marigold needed to find a worthy man and set up her own household. He was a loner, who, at that moment, couldn't talk himself into staying alone.

"May I come in?" he asked.

The girls nodded. Marigold gave him a smile.

"How's the ankle?" he asked, then realized asking about a lady's limb was indelicate.

Marigold grimaced. "Sprained. I can't walk on it for days."

"You mean you'll have to let others do for you?" Gordon couldn't stop himself from grinning.

"Yes, a maidservant who can't serve." Her eyes twinkled. "Maybe I should go home."

"Do you want to?" His alarm startled him.

Her, too, for her eyes widened, and her lips parted without a sound emerging.

"It's all right if you do," he added more calmly.

"I don't want to leave the girls right now."

Right now. That meant one day she would, leave the girls, leave him.

Gordon pulled up a footstool and sat facing the ladies. "Well then, let's get this over with." He focused his attention on Ruby. "Why did you run away this morning?"

"I dunno." She popped her fingers into her mouth, then yanked them out again, squared her shoulders, and looked him in the eye. "I don't want to be afraid of the water and be a baby."

"So you stowed away on a boat to prove you're not afraid?" Gordon questioned with an effort around the unfortunate tendency of his lips twitching. "You didn't think that was naughty?"

"Yes, it was naughty." She hung her head. "And now you're going to go away again because I was naughty like when Mommy and Daddy went away."

"Died," Beryl interjected.

Ruby nodded. "Yes, died."

A strangled sound from Marigold drew Gordon's attention to her. She held her hand to her lips, and tears filled her bright eyes. Ruby's words sank in, and his own throat tightened.

"What does you being naughty and your parents' accident have to do with each other?" Gordon made himself ask.

Ruby started to cry, harsh, racking sobs. "Because I was always naughty."

Gordon crouched before her.

He removed his handkerchief from his pocket and began to wipe her cheeks. "Of course you were naughty. Children are naughty. Adults are naughty."

"But I made Mommy and Daddy go away," Ruby wailed. "Forever."

Gordon glanced at Marigold for help in understanding what Ruby was talking about. Marigold shook her head.

"How could you make them go away forever?" Gordon asked.

Ruby took his handkerchief and cried into it.

"She left her doll out in the rain the day before, and that day she broke Daddy's picture of Mommy," Beryl said. "Daddy yelled at her and sent her to her room. Mommy said it wasn't a good picture and she didn't like it anyway and. . ." Her lower lip quivered. "They started to argue."

"They weren't arguing when they left." Marigold spoke up for the first time. "They looked quite happy with one another when they greeted me on their way out."

"You told me to stay in the nursery," Ruby said. "But I sneaked down to Mommy and Daddy's room to look at their pretty things."

Beryl slumped in her chair. "I didn't try to stop her. I wanted her to get into trouble because—because everyone thinks I have to be a good example to her, and they thought every time she did something wrong it was my fault. Mommy told me I should have gotten Ruby's doll from the lawn if I knew it was there. But this time it wasn't. It was hers."

"I know," Ruby wailed.

"No, I didn't mean that. Oh, Ruby." Beryl slid from the sofa and wrapped one arm around her sister's shoulders. "I didn't mean Mommy and Daddy going away. I mean I didn't have anything to do with it. You got into trouble all by yourself, like this morning."

"And now Uncle Gordon will go away forever," Ruby sobbed.

Gordon had gone days without speaking to another soul. He didn't mind the silence or his lack of facility with words—until there in the parlor with his niece. He looked to Marigold for help. She seemed to always have a great deal to say. But she shook her head and refused to meet his eyes.

He cleared his throat. He needed to speak. Ruby was his responsibility. He couldn't depend on anyone else to heal her heart, as much as he wanted to remain aloof, remote, out of trouble with his heart.

"I was going to go away even before I met you, Ruby," he began. "If—I mean, when I leave, it will have nothing to do with you being naughty."

"What if I'm especially good?" Ruby peeked at him above the broad handkerchief. "Will you stay? You know, if I don't suck my fingers and I'm not afraid of water?"

"And if I stop being mean to Ruby and calling her a baby and things like that?" Beryl added.

"I. . .um. . ." Gordon glanced around the room, as though an easy answer would spring forth from one of the dozens of books lining the walls. "I prefer to be alone."

"Why?" the girls asked.

"So I don't hurt people who love me." He spoke the truth for the first time to anyone, yet the confusion and sadness on his nieces' faces told him he was hurting them by planning to leave.

"I'm not leaving right away," he concluded.

"Then we can pers—pers—get you to stay?" Ruby asked, her eyes brightening.

"If I stay," Gordon said, "it won't be because you're naughty or good. It will be because—because—"

"Maybe God wants you to stay," Beryl suggested.

"He's certainly seen to it your inheritance is worthless for now," Marigold murmured.

Minx. She was a proud, wild-haired, outspoken minx.

And if he stayed, it was because he was in love with her.

"Let's pray and see what God tells us." Gordon rose. "I have to take care of the business right now, make sure my orders are being carried out, and reassure the workers they'll be paid. While I'm gone, I want you girls to come up with all the reasons why you should never leave the house without permission."

"But I didn't—" Beryl clapped her hand over her mouth. "I'll write them down."

"Good girl." Gordon tugged a pigtail on each girl. "Keep close watch on them. I shouldn't be long."

"Where are you going?" Marigold asked.

Minx indeed. No employee should ask that of her employer.

"I'm going to the boathouse to dismiss Lawrence Randall and ensure none of those boats go out again until I'm satisfied they're all seaworthy."

"That'll take months," Marigold said, her eyes narrowed.

"Months," he agreed. "But if he'll stay on, I'm hiring Dennis Tripp to oversee the operation. Do you know an honest bookkeeper? I suspect those clerks knew what Randall was up to and helped him cover up his accounting."

"I might," Marigold said and grinned.

"I'd have mutiny if I hired a female accountant," he said, grinning himself, though he felt foolish.

fifteen

A week later, when Marigold heard Gordon return to the house, she descended the steps, albeit still stiffly, to find him. The girls were working on their math, though giggling far more than the assignment warranted. She did nothing to stop the hilarity. Hearing them laugh, like little girls should, eased a burden from her heart.

Gordon had eased a burden from the girls' hearts—for the time being. If he departed, he would hurt them nearly as deeply as had the death of their parents, convincing them their naughtiness—far more mild than the pranks Marigold had gotten into as a girl—had caused the losses in their lives.

She found Gordon in the library. He stood at the window, his back to the room, his shoulders slumped, his head bowed, as she had seen him too often before. His knuckles gleamed white he gripped the windowsill so tightly.

Marigold hesitated in the doorway then marched up to him and laid one of her hands over his. "What's happened?"

"I'm just feeling guilty about all the trouble with the excursion company. Dennis is doing well getting matters under way, and Randall didn't steal all the money." He snorted. "I suppose he had a certain honor. He only took the money he claimed he was spending on repairs."

"And no one's found him?" Marigold knew the answer.

"Not yet, but I expect they will. The West isn't as easy to hide in as it once was. We were even getting telephones in some places."

"Civilization has its advantages." She tried to smile.

Talk of civilization reminded her of how much he wanted away from it.

"I've come up with a way to set up the ledgers for the company," she said.

"And I suppose I will have to abide by them, or you'll badger me to death." His smile took the sting from his words.

It removed any protective coating from her heart that might have remained.

"I am a bit of a managing female except that I—" She bit her lower lip and closed her eyes.

An endless succession of *I*s floated across the inside of her eyelids then settled onto her shoulders like a leaden cloak.

"I'm not very good at managing anything," she concluded in a whisper.

"You've done remarkably well, considering the circumstances my selfishness left you in." Gordon faced her and touched her cheek with the tips of his fingers, a caress as light as a breeze, as powerful as a hurricane.

She jumped, and their gazes collided. The tenderness she saw in his smashed the last vestiges of her pride.

"How can you think well of me?" Her voice emerged in a whisper. "I missed that the ledgers were in code. Your nieces have been so unhappy they misbehave when they used to be good children. I embarrassed you in front of neighbors. Then I sprained my ankle when you needed me most. And now—"

Now, the worst humiliation would be to tell him she was in love with him and not mourning her fiancé at all.

God, what are You trying to tell me?

But of course she knew the answer to that. She wasn't supposed to be the one who solved everyone's problems. She was supposed to depend on the Lord to solve them.

She backed away from Gordon, far enough away he couldn't reach out to her. Far enough away she couldn't catch his scent of sun-dried linens and a lemony soap. She would have to leave the room to be far enough away not to look into his dark but sparkling eyes.

"I shouldn't have come back," she said. "I should have stayed in Hudson City with my family and faced the fact that God's plan for my life isn't to make everything right for others. You have to make them right for yourself."

"I don't want you to leave," Gordon said. "I need you to stay and be as managing as you like."

"So you can leave as quickly as possible? I can't let you—"

Gordon started to laugh. Marigold glared at him for a moment, then as the reality of her words sank in, she laughed, too.

"So if I leave, I'm forcing you to stay." She stifled another fit of giggles, and unsuccessfully tried to stifle a different kind of fit—a wish to fling her arms around Gordon and tell him to laugh again so she could see his eyes dance.

She reached out to him instead, though she had stepped too far away to touch him. "Why do you want to leave us—I mean your family? Surely the past is behind you, whatever made you leave in the first place."

"I had hopes that it was." He began to pace around the library, laying a hand on his desk then his other hand on a vase sporting a spray of marigolds atop the mantel. "My father sent me away because I was so selfish I tended to hurt others without realizing it or, too often, caring that I had. The last straw—" He faced her. "Marigold, will you walk down to the boathouse with me? Is your ankle up to it?"

She would have walked to New York City on her sprained ankle if he asked her.

"Yes. But the girls—"

"Without the girls. Mrs. Cromwell can watch them. I need to get some supplies ordered for Dennis. . .and other things."

"All right. I'll be back in five minutes."

"Make that at least a quarter hour."

"It won't take me that long to tell Mrs. Cromwell we're stepping out and to get a hat."

"But it will take you that long to change out of that ugly dress."

She stared at him. "You don't like my dress?"

"I detest it." One corner of his mouth tilted up. "In fact, as your employer and your friend, I'm requesting you never wear it again."

And his friend.

The words lent wings to Marigold's feet. She raced into the kitchen to tell Mrs. Cromwell she would be gone with Mr. Chambers for a while, then charged up to her room to yank off the ugly dress. Buttons flew in all directions. She let them fly. The gown would make excellent rags for cleaning brass.

Beryl came in while Marigold was struggling to button up the back of a muslin gown sprigged with tiny purple flowers. "Are you angry, Miss Marigold? We're being good."

"You're being angels." Marigold hugged the child. "And, no, I'm not angry. I'm going for a walk and need something nicer to wear is all."

"Can we go, too?" Ruby asked from the doorway.

"Not this time. It's business."

"You look too happy for business," Ruby observed.

Beryl tilted her head to one side. "Are you going alone?"

"No." Her cheeks warm, Marigold plopped a hat onto her head and skewered it into place with a pearl-headed pin. Curls tumbled over her ears, but she left them alone.

Her fifteen minutes were up.

"If you're finished with your arithmetic," she told the children, "you may play in the yard or read out there, but I want you outdoors for a little while. Mrs. Cromwell will give you some lemonade."

"Is Uncle Gordon going with you?" Ruby persisted.

"We're going down to the boathouse."

"I want to come," Ruby said.

"Not this time. We need to talk about grown-up business."

Not the business Marigold thought they should talk about, the business she wanted to talk about—why she wanted him to stay. He would have to figure that out on his own. She wasn't laying her pride on the line with a man again.

She descended the steps and joined Gordon on the front

porch. She didn't need to ask if her gown was acceptable; his glance said it all.

He offered her his arm. "Let's walk. I want to talk to you."

"About me leaving your employment? About you hiring me to do your bookkeeping instead of—"

"About me."

She winced. She would have to add *me* to all the *I* pronouns that pricked her conscience with their implication of self-centered behavior and thinking.

"I need to tell you why I left Cape May." Gordon set out at a leisurely pace that didn't strain her ankle. "Then you can decide. . . ."

He didn't say what he thought she could decide. She didn't ask. She waited for him to speak.

"I thought I was helping. . .someone." He passed the walkway leading to the boathouse and directed their steps to the boardwalk. "It was a young lady. Well, most considered her a maidservant, not a lady, but she was soft-spoken and polite and—she acted like a lady."

"Unlike me." Marigold tried to ease the tension she felt radiating through his fingers.

He smiled faintly. "As to the soft-spoken part, yes, different from you, but you're a lady, Marigold. Never doubt that."

"Thank you. Go on, if you must."

"I must. You need to understand why I found coming back so difficult, why being here has been difficult for me."

"You owe me no explanations."

He covered her hand where it rested on his forearm. "Don't I? I thought. . . Perhaps I was wrong. I don't trust my own judgment much, and it's difficult learning to rely on the Lord to direct me."

"I do understand." She smiled. "I'm better at directing the Lord. But go on. Tell me about this lady."

And let her heart break, if he'd been hopelessly in love, if he still loved.

They strolled along in silence for several moments, with the sea and sun spread out beside them in blue and gold splendor. Then Gordon took a deep breath and began. "She worked for us. She was a maid. She was a fine girl, but her brother wasn't a good man. He kept coming around and stealing her wages and trying to get her to make more by dishonest means like stealing from us. But he stole from us, and she was going to be arrested. My father didn't tolerate rule breaking of any kind."

"Oh, no, that's so unfair."

"It happens too often, you know. I had a bit of a soft heart for her. No, it was more than that. I'd fallen for her prettiness, her sweetness, though my father always warned us to not even make friends with the maids, for the sake of propriety and, I suppose, because he didn't think they were good wife prospects."

"My great-grandmother was a maid. And I—"

"Have never been a maid, whatever work you've done." He smiled down at her and laced his fingers through hers. "But Louisa was. I bought her ice cream a time or two and some chocolates. It was all innocent from beginning to end. I was barely eighteen and she the same." He fell silent, his face pensive.

Marigold's gut tightened with the realization that he recalled another maid, another female, one who had indeed held his heart even a little.

Another stab to her pride that he would think of another female with such depth while he was with her.

She remained silent, waiting for him to continue speaking.

"I helped her escape from being arrested," he said abruptly.

"You did? Gordon—I mean, Mr. Chambers, that was very bad of you."

"I didn't think she'd go free if they arrested her, so I used my position as heir apparent to the boating business to take out one of the boats. I got her aboard without anyone knowing and intended to sail her across the Delaware Bay to Philadelphia. She could have gotten a train to anywhere from there, gone out West, and found a new life without anyone knowing the better for it." He sighed and turned his face to the sea. "But I failed. It was the only sailboat we had, and I capsized it. She couldn't swim."

Marigold stumbled. "She didn't—didn't—"

"No, she didn't drown. I got her to shore, but we were alone for a long time until someone rescued us, and on top of being accused of stealing, her reputation was further ruined. And it was my fault."

"But your intentions were good." Marigold's heart ached for the kindhearted boy.

"My intentions were selfish, Marigold." And his tone was harsh. "My father had often accused me of not ever thinking of others, so I wanted to prove I did. Except I really didn't. I did it for my own reasons and harmed her in the end."

"What reasons?"

"That I was man enough to take care of myself and others—that I deserved to run the excursion company. . . I'm not certain I know any longer."

"But—" Marigold stopped and instead of pressing him further, inquired, "What happened to her?"

"My father dropped the charges against her so I wouldn't be complicit in her crime, then he found her work in another city. He didn't tell me where."

"Then she got away from her brother."

"She did, but she also got stuck right back into a situation where something similar could happen to her. And the new people knew her background, so I doubt it was comfortable for her."

"You don't know?"

"No."

"But—" Marigold stopped again, words failing her except for the next question she didn't think she should ask.

They had reached the lighthouse. Gordon stopped and leaned against its white-painted wall, away from the door where people streamed in and out.

"My father said I'd abused my position of authority with

the company to do harm, not good, and disinherited me. I thought my brother, my twin, would support me. He sided with Father, called me a fool. An irresponsible fool." He looked away toward a flock of seagulls diving for food on the sand. "Gerald was a good man, but he was business-minded like Father, and that scandal was bound to hurt some of his connections. So I left the next day and never came home again."

"Why?" Marigold could hold back no longer. "I don't mean why would your father do that? I expect he'd get over his anger and change his will back, unless he was a tyrant, so why did you leave and never come home? Didn't you miss your family? Didn't you miss having a home and friends and the same church every Sunday?"

"Every single day. But every time I let myself be too friendly with someone, I seemed to interfere somehow, making matters worse. I decided that I'm better off alone."

"Because you can't fix everyone's problems, either?" Marigold grinned at him.

He grinned back.

Marigold wanted to hold the moment, but she needed to hear everything from him, from past actions to future plans. "So you were afraid to come home for three months, even though you were needed here."

"Yes, but now I see that I have to let the Lord guide me through, to take the risk with His help. If I leave now, I'll hurt the girls and those depending on me for work at the excursion company, and I want to stay, especially if—but I cost you your fiancé, your wedding, your inheritance."

"Yes, to the inheritance, but it's just a piece of glass. A glass with sentiment and meaning behind it, but a piece of glass— nothing more." Marigold smiled. "And as for the fiancé, I'd say your delay saved me. If he couldn't wait for me for a little while longer, how much could he have loved me? That's a marriage I didn't need."

"You believe that? I mean—" He stared down at the toes

of his shoes, up to the top of the lighthouse's flame—nearly invisible in the daylight—and not quite into her eyes. "Your heart isn't broken?"

"On the contrary." Marigold's heart raced like a colt in a derby. She now knew what she needed to say, but if she was wrong, if his feelings for her didn't run deeply, she would face the worst humiliation of her life. Without the risk to her pride, though, she would gain nothing.

She started to take his hands again, then stepped closer and rested her hands on his broad shoulders. "Gordon, in these past weeks, I've come to realize that I—that I—" Her throat went so dry she could scarcely talk. "I convinced myself that I loved Lucian because I wanted to get married and he offered for me. But when I met you, something happened to me. I stopped thinking about him, even before I knew there was no hope of getting him back, and. . . . Trying to persuade you to stay wasn't wholly for the sake of the girls. And coming back here after my sister's wedding wasn't all because I didn't like the humiliation of everyone knowing I'd been abandoned. Even though that was part of it." She laughed. "If my father wanted to teach me humility, he should have just bribed Lucian to jilt me publicly, instead of making me work for a year. But I'm glad he did. I found you here. If you leave for Alaska, I'll probably follow you."

"Marigold, are you saying—" The afternoon sunshine lit his features as though the lighthouse flame burned from within him. He clasped her shoulders then cupped her face in his hands. "Are you saying you care for me?"

"I'm saying that I love you." Words tumbled from her lips. "It's all right if you don't love me, too. I just had to tell you so you wouldn't think your staying away had hurt me or ruined my future somehow. But don't think you're hurting me if you don't feel the same—"

He pressed his forefinger to her lips. "Marigold, please be quiet." He replaced his finger with his mouth, kissing her longer, more deeply than he had before. Long enough to draw a crowd of appreciative onlookers. Long enough for Marigold to grow too breathless to even think of speaking. And amid the cheers and congratulations of the vacationers, Gordon raised his head for the moment it took him to say, "I love you, too."

epilogue

Cape May, New Jersey
June 1900

Marigold and Gordon waited nearly eight months to marry—eight months in which they worked long days and into a few evenings to restore the business. As Gordon's bookkeeper and not his nieces' nursemaid, Marigold moved down the street to the Morris house, where one of their widowed cousins lived with her for propriety. So close to Gordon and the girls, Marigold managed to spend a great deal of time at their house, trying—and often succeeding—not to interfere with the girls' governess and Mrs. Cromwell's replacement.

Though Marigold worked with Gordon, she didn't see that much of him during the day. She spent her days in Randall's old office unraveling the man's ledgers and setting up a new bookkeeping system. Gordon worked with Dennis Tripp and some other employees, inspecting and repairing the boats and converting two of them into craft able to carry supplies across the bay, to increase the company's productivity even more than Gerald had begun to do.

By Easter the books were in order and two reliable clerks were hired to replace the ones who had disappeared along with Lawrence Randall, who had yet to be found. So Marigold went home to plan her wedding.

The weeks dragged by without Gordon, without Ruby and Beryl, without daily work. But at last, her family in tow, Marigold returned to Cape May to discover Gordon had conspired with her mother about one wedding arrangement.

"We're getting married on a boat?" Marigold exclaimed.

"Unless you object." Gordon held her hands as though never intending to let them go. "I'm sure I can talk the pastor into letting us have the church, but your mother and I have made all the arrangements."

"I don't object." Gazing into his root beer–colored eyes, Marigold feared she would agree to anything he said. "I'm just surprised. It's so. . .romantic."

"We're getting dozens and dozens of roses in." Ruby scampered into the library, braids escaping from their pink ribbons.

Beryl followed, neat and clean in her sky blue dress. "Not dozens and dozens. Well, maybe." She grinned.

"Roses?" Marigold shuddered. "But—"

"White ones," he assured her, "so they don't rival your hair."

Marigold laughed and hugged him.

"Tomorrow," he assured her, setting her from him with gentle firmness. "After tomorrow, we don't have to say good night and part."

"Tomorrow won't come fast enough."

But her mother and sister made plans that would hasten the time. She needed one more fitting for her dress. She needed to wash her hair, so it had time to dry before bed. She had gifts to unwrap.

"Shouldn't Gordon be with me? And the girls wanted to be with me for the present-opening," she protested as they set her down amid her bridesmaids and a pile of packages tied up with white satin bows.

"Not for these." The bridesmaids, friends from college, giggled.

Marigold blushed, guessing that the parcels held delicate undergarments. She opened each box, sighed over the fine silks and intricate lace, then tried to rise, suddenly desperate for sleep to bring the next day faster.

"One more." Rose, not in the wedding because she was expecting her first child, sank to her knees before Marigold. "This is from me."

"But you and Adam already gave me that lovely tea service," Marigold protested.

"Yes, from Adam and me. This is just from me." Rose set a small box on Marigold's lap but didn't let go of it.

A rustling filled the room, then silence followed. Marigold glanced up to see the last of her friends whisking away.

"Why are they leaving?" Marigold asked, her stomach suddenly uneasy.

Rose smiled. "Because I asked them to. This is special. Between us."

Marigold's heart skipped a beat. "You're my sister, my best friend. I don't need more from you than that."

"I know, but you gave me so much. You sacrificed so much last year, staying here to take care of the girls, losing Lucian."

"No loss."

Lucian had broken his engagement to the Grassick girl and left New Jersey for parts unknown. He'd proven Father to be right in thinking that young man had too little of a sense of responsibility to be a good spouse.

"Maybe he wasn't a good catch," Rose said, "but it hurt you to see me marry first."

"I deserved it after being so awful to you."

"You were awful, but it's forgiven. I forgave you a long time before I even met Adam. Our friendship is too important for me to hold a grudge."

"Thank you. That's the most precious gift you could give me."

"Then let me seal it with this." Rose pushed the box more firmly into Marigold's hands.

"If you insist." She peeled back the wrapping.

Even before she opened the lid, she knew what the box contained.

It was the glass goldfinch, once again a gift of love and constancy.

A Letter To Our Readers

Dear Reader:

In order that we might better contribute to your reading enjoyment, we would appreciate your taking a few minutes to respond to the following questions. We welcome your comments and read each form and letter we receive. When completed, please return to the following:

Fiction Editor
Heartsong Presents
PO Box 719
Uhrichsville, Ohio 44683

1. Did you enjoy reading *The Newcomer* by Laurie Alice Eakes?
   ❑ Very much! I would like to see more books by this author!
   ❑ Moderately. I would have enjoyed it more if

   _____

   _____

   _____

2. Are you a member of **Heartsong Presents**? ❑ Yes ❑ No
   If no, where did you purchase this book? _____

   _____

3. How would you rate, on a scale from 1 (poor) to 5 (superior), the cover design? _____

4. On a scale from 1 (poor) to 10 (superior), please rate the following elements.

   ____ Heroine   ____ Plot
   ____ Hero   ____ Inspirational theme
   ____ Setting   ____ Secondary characters

5. These characters were special because? _____
_____
_____

6. How has this book inspired your life? _____
_____
_____

7. What settings would you like to see covered in future
   Heartsong Presents books? _____
_____
_____

8. What are some inspirational themes you would like to see
   treated in future books? _____
_____
_____

9. Would you be interested in reading other **Heartsong
   Presents** titles? ❏ Yes ❏ No

10. Please check your age range:
    ❏ Under 18   ❏ 18-24
    ❏ 25-34   ❏ 35-45
    ❏ 46-55   ❏ Over 55

Name _____
Occupation _____
Address _____
City, State, Zip _____
E-mail _____

SEASIDE ROMANCE

3 stories in 1

Finding their true loves requires daring leaps of faith for each of three women from Rhode Island's seaside communities of old.

Historical, paperback, 352 pages, 5¾₆" x 8"

Heartsong

HEARTSONG PRESENTS TITLES AVAILABLE NOW:

___HP683 *A Gentlemen's Kiss*, K. Comeaux
___HP684 *Copper Sunrise*, C. Cox
___HP687 *The Ruse*, T. H. Murray
___HP688 *A Handful of Flowers*, C. M. Hake
___HP691 *Bayou Dreams*, K. M. Y'Barbo
___HP692 *The Oregon Escort*, S. P. Davis
___HP695 *Into the Deep*, L. Bliss
___HP696 *Bridal Veil*, C. M. Hake
___HP699 *Bittersweet Remembrance*, G. Fields
___HP700 *Where the River Flows*, I. Brand
___HP703 *Moving the Mountain*, Y. Lehman
___HP704 *No Buttons or Beaux*, C. M. Hake
___HP707 *Mariah's Hope*, M. J. Conner
___HP708 *The Prisoner's Wife*, S. P. Davis
___HP711 *A Gentle Fragrance*, P. Griffin
___HP712 *Spoke of Love*, C. M. Hake
___HP715 *Vera's Turn for Love*, T. H. Murray
___HP716 *Spinning Out of Control*,
    V. McDonough
___HP719 *Weaving a Future*, S. P. Davis
___HP720 *Bridge Across the Sea*, P. Griffin
___HP723 *Adam's Bride*, L. Harris
___HP724 *A Daughter's Quest*, L. N. Dooley
___HP727 *Wyoming Hoofbeats*, S. P. Davis
___HP728 *A Place of Her Own*, L. A. Coleman
___HP731 *The Bounty Hunter and the Bride*,
    V. McDonough
___HP732 *Lonely in Longtree*, J. Stengl
___HP735 *Deborah*, M. Colvin
___HP736 *A Time to Plant*, K. E. Hake
___HP740 *The Castaway's Bride*, S. P. Davis
___HP741 *Golden Dawn*, C. M. Hake
___HP743 *Broken Bow*, I. Brand
___HP744 *Golden Days*, M. Connealy
___HP747 *A Wealth Beyond Riches*,
    V. McDonough

___HP748 *Golden Twilight*, K. Y'Barbo
___HP751 *The Music of Home*, T. H. Murray
___HP752 *Tara's Gold*, L. Harris
___HP755 *Journey to Love*, L. Bliss
___HP756 *The Lumberjack's Lady*, S. P. Davis
___HP759 *Stirring Up Romance*, J. L. Barton
___HP760 *Mountains Stand Strong*, I. Brand
___HP763 *A Time to Keep*, K. E. Hake
___HP764 *To Trust an Outlaw*, R. Gibson
___HP767 *A Bride Idea*, Y. Lehman
___HP768 *Sharon Takes a Hand*, R. Dow
___HP771 *Canteen Dreams*, C. Putman
___HP772 *Corduroy Road to Love*, L. A. Coleman
___HP775 *Treasure in the Hills*, P. W. Dooly
___HP776 *Betsy's Return*, W. E. Brunstetter
___HP779 *Joanna's Adventure*, M. J. Conner
___HP780 *The Dreams of Hannah Williams*,
    L. Ford
___HP783 *Seneca Shadows*, L. Bliss
___HP784 *Promises, Promises*, A. Miller
___HP787 *A Time to Laugh*, K. Hake
___HP788 *Uncertain Alliance*, M. Davis
___HP791 *Better Than Gold*, L. A. Eakes
___HP792 *Sweet Forever*, R. Cecil
___HP795 *A Treasure Reborn*, P. Griffin
___HP796 *The Captain's Wife*, M. Davis
___HP799 *Sandhill Dreams*, C. C. Putman
___HP800 *Return to Love*, S. P. Davis
___HP803 *Quills and Promises*, A. Miller
___HP804 *Reckless Rogue*, M. Davis
___HP807 *The Greatest Find*, P. W. Dooly
___HP808 *The Long Road Home*, R. Druten
___HP811 *A New Joy*, S.P. Davis
___HP812 *Everlasting Promise*, R.K. Cecil
___HP815 *A Treasure Regained*, P. Griffin
___HP816 *Wild at Heart*, V. McDonough

(If ordering from this page, please remember to include it with the order form.)

Presents

___HP819 *Captive Dreams*, C. C. Putman
___HP820 *Carousel Dreams*, P. W. Dooly
___HP823 *Deceptive Promises*, A. Miller
___HP824 *Alias, Mary Smith*, R. Druten
___HP827 *Abiding Peace*, S. P. Davis
___HP828 *A Season for Grace*, T. Bateman
___HP831 *Outlaw Heart*, V. McDonough
___HP832 *Charity's Heart*, R. K. Cecil
___HP835 *A Treasure Revealed*, P. Griffin
___HP836 *A Love for Keeps*, J. L. Barton
___HP839 *Out of the Ashes*, R. Druten
___HP840 *The Petticoat Doctor*, P. W. Dooly
___HP843 *Copper and Candles*, A. Stockton
___HP844 *Aloha Love*, Y. Lehman
___HP847 *A Girl Like That*, F. Devine
___HP848 *Remembrance*, J. Spaeth
___HP851 *Straight for the Heart*, V. McDonough
___HP852 *A Love All Her Own*, J. L. Barton
___HP855 *Beacon of Love*, D. Franklin
___HP856 *A Promise Kept*, C. C. Putman
___HP859 *The Master's Match*, T. H. Murray
___HP860 *Under the Tulip Poplar*, D. Ashley &
      A. McCarver
___HP863 *All that Glitters*, L. Sowell
___HP864 *Picture Bride*, Y. Lehman
___HP867 *Hearts and Harvest*, A. Stockton
___HP868 *A Love to Cherish*, J. L. Barton

___HP871 *Once a Thief*, F. Devine
___HP872 *Kind-Hearted Woman*, J. Spaeth
___HP875 *The Bartered Bride*, E. Vetsch
___HP876 *A Promise Born*, C. C. Putman
___HP877 *A Still, Small Voice*, K. O'Brien
___HP878 *Opie's Challenge*, T. Fowler
___HP879 *A Bouquet for Iris*, D. Ashley &
      A. McCarver
___HP880 *The Glassblower*, L.A. Eakes
___HP883 *Patterns and Progress*, A. Stockton
___HP884 *Love From Ashes*, Y. Lehman
___HP887 *The Marriage Masquerade*, E. Vetsch
___HP888 *In Search of a Memory*, P. Griffin
___HP891 *Sugar and Spice*, F. Devine
___HP892 *The Mockingbird's Call*, D. Ashley and
      A. McCarver
___HP895 *The Ice Carnival*, J. Spaeth
___HP896 *A Promise Forged*, C. C. Putman
___HP899 *The Heiress*, L. A. Eakes
___HP900 *Clara and the Cowboy*, E. Vetsch
___HP903 *The Lightkeeper's Daughter*, P. W. Dooly
___HP904 *Romance Rides the Range*, C. Reece
___HP907 *The Engineered Engagement*, E. Vetsch
___HP908 *In Search of a Dream*, P. Griffin
___HP911 *The Prodigal Patriot*, D. Franklin
___HP912 *Promise of Tomorrow*, S. D. Moore

Great Inspirational Romance at a Great Price!

Heartsong Presents books are inspirational romances in
contemporary and historical settings, designed to give you an
enjoyable, spirit-lifting reading experience. You can choose
wonderfully written titles from some of today's best authors like
Wanda E. Brunstetter, Mary Connealy, Susan Page Davis,
Cathy Marie Hake, Joyce Livingston, and many others.

When ordering quantities less than twelve, above titles are $2.97 each.
Not all titles may be available at time of order.